ONLY IF YOU DARE

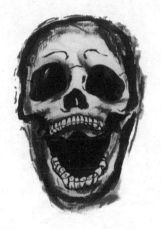

ONLY IF YOU DARE

13 STORIES OF DARKNESS AND DOOM

by

JOSH ALLEN

illustrated by

SARAH J. COLEMAN

HOLIDAY HOUSE · NEW YORK

Text copyright © 2021 by Josh Allen
Illustrations copyright © 2021 by Sarah J. Coleman
All Rights Reserved
HOLIDAY HOUSE is registered in the U.S. Patent and Trademark Office.
Printed and bound in June 2021 at Maple Press, York, PA, USA.
www.holidayhouse.com
First Edition
1 3 5 7 9 10 8 6 4 2

Library of Congress Cataloging-in-Publication Data

Names: Allen, Josh, author. | Coleman, Sarah (Sarah Jane), illustrator.
Title: Only if you dare : 13 stories of darkness and doom / by Josh Allen ;
illustrated by Sarah J. Coleman.
Description: New York : Holiday House, [2021] | Audience: Ages 9–12.
Audience: Grades 4–6. | Summary: A collection of thirteen short stories
showing how horribly wrong food, dating, jobs, and even a bed pillow can be.
Identifiers: LCCN 2020035167 | ISBN 9780823449064 (hardcover)
Subjects: LCSH: Horror tales, American. | Children's stories, American.
CYAC: Horror stories. | Short stories.
Classification: LCC PZ7.1.A4387 Onl 2021 | DDC [Fic]—dc23
LC record available at https://lccn.loc.gov/2020035167

ISBN: 978-0-8234-4906-4 (hardcover)

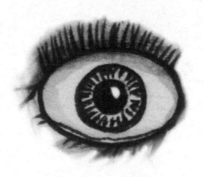

FOR MOM AND DAD.
AND FOR EVERYONE ELSE
WHO IS BRAVE ENOUGH.

CONTENTS

THE SUBSTITUTE   1

THE PERFECT GIRL   18

LUMPY, LUMPY   38

HI, JENNY.   50

CRAZY PLAYZ   71

THE SNOWMAN WHO WOULDN'T MELT   89

SCRABBLED   102

MY HAND, RIGHT THERE   116

WAKE UP!   130

WE ALL SCREAM FOR ICE CREAM   145

ONE OF A KIND   160

ONE MORE PIECE   175

THE HEARTBEAT: A BEDTIME STORY   195

the Substitute

I T was October 31, Halloween, and Hazel walked into life science class a few minutes early. Only, Ms. Jacobson wasn't in her usual spot next to the whiteboards. Instead, a thin man with a long black beard stood in her place.

"A substitute," Hazel whispered as she slid into her seat next to Ava, her best friend.

But she'd never seen a substitute like this before.

For one thing, the man at the front of the class was wearing a suit. A black one. With a black tie and shiny black shoes. None of the teachers at Tidewater Middle School, not even the substitutes, ever wore suits.

Maybe it's a Halloween costume, Hazel thought.

And then there was that beard. It went halfway down his chest.

The substitute didn't look up as students trickled in. He didn't say *hello* or *good morning*. He just stood there beside Ms. Jacobson's desk reading a dusty book.

Hazel shrugged at Ava and raised her eyebrows. Maybe, Hazel figured, all these things—the suit, the tie, the silent reading—had nothing to do with Halloween. Maybe they were substitute-teacher tricks to keep everyone from trying to get away with anything.

When the bell rang, the substitute closed his dusty book and set it on Ms. Jacobson's desk. Then he ran his fingers through his beard. Finally, he spoke.

"Did you know," he said in a high, quiet voice, "that octopuses have three hearts?"

Hazel blinked. Around her, no one said anything. Everyone's faces were scrunched. She turned to Ava, who'd begun tapping her pencil on her desk.

"And snails have teeth," the substitute said. He walked back and forth across the front of the room. His polished shoes made light tapping sounds on the floor. "In fact, snails have thousands of teeth. Some of them, as many as fourteen thousand."

There was a pause. Students started to whisper.

"What's going on?" said Miguel Rodriguez.

"Who is this guy?" hissed Sheryl Jones from the back row.

"Is this a Halloween thing?" said Noah Haight.

Hazel turned again to Ava and saw that her best friend's eyes had narrowed. Ava, Hazel knew, hated Halloween. Haunted houses, spooky movies, scary pranks. She didn't like any of it. She called Halloween "the worst of all holidays." If this was a Halloween thing, Ava wasn't going to like it. Not a bit.

"Bats," the substitute continued, "are the only mammals that can fly."

Bats, Hazel thought. *So this is a Halloween thing.*

She raised her hand.

"Excuse me," she said. "But who are you, exactly?"

A few kids chuckled.

"I'm your substitute," the bearded man said. "My name is Walter Fernsby, but I guess you should call me Mr. Fernsby."

Walter Fernsby, Hazel thought. *That's an old person's name.*

But the substitute didn't look old. He had smooth pale skin and straight white teeth.

He lifted a blue binder off Ms. Jacobson's desk and held it up. "I see here," he said, waggling the binder, "that Ms. Jacobson would like me to teach you a lesson today on the different parts of cells."

He put the binder down.

"But," he said leaning forward and dropping his voice, "I'll bet you've had loads of lessons on cells before."

He smiled.

Hazel tilted her head. It was true that she'd probably sat through dozens of lessons on cells, or hundreds, even. But what was the substitute's point? Where was he going with this?

Hazel looked up and down the rows of her classmates. Around her, there was a buzz in the air. An excitement. It was Halloween, and *something* was happening. *Something different.* A few desks over, Miguel Rodriguez was actually smiling. In the front row, Noah Haight was sitting up. Even Mari Kuniyuki had switched off her cell phone and set it in front of her.

Next to Hazel, though, Ava was still tapping her pencil on her desk. Last Halloween, she and Ava had gone to one of those haunted corn mazes, and Ava had started crying after five minutes. She'd ended up sitting on the ground with her eyes shut tight and her hands clamped over her ears.

Hazel had put her arms around Ava and walked her out.

And sometimes when the two girls watched movies together, Ava would close her eyes in the middle of a scary part and say, *Tell me when it's over.*

Hazel would always make sure everything was safe before she'd say, *It's fine now, Ava. You can look.*

"Well, since I am a substitute teacher," Mr. Fernsby went on, "I thought that today I might teach you a substitute lesson."

In the next desk over, Ava raised her hand. "Can you please just teach us about cells?" she said.

Hazel thought she heard a slight quiver in Ava's voice.

The substitute didn't answer. He took a few steps across the front of the room. He seemed to be waiting for something.

"What's the substitute lesson about?" Noah Haight asked. He was leaning forward with his elbows on his desk.

Mr. Fernsby looked around the room and made eye contact with a few students.

"The substitute lesson is about . . . *Them*," he said, and the way he said the word *Them*, slow and looming and with a bit of a growl, made Hazel open her mouth slightly.

She turned to Ava. "It'll be okay," she whispered.

"Who are *Them?*" said Sheryl Jones from the back row.

"*Them* are the biggest mystery in all of life science," Mr. Fernsby said. "*Them* are creatures, stranger even than the three-hearted octopus, the thousand-toothed snail, and the flying-mammal bat all put together. *Them* are much more . . . monstrous."

Mr. Fernsby stroked his black beard with one hand. A Halloween eeriness filled the room.

Hazel checked Ava again. Her pencil-tapping had become faster.

Did Ms. Jacobson arrange this? Hazel wondered. A Halloween prank didn't seem like something she would do.

Hazel squinted at Mr. Fernsby.

"Are you talking about snakes or something?" said Miguel Rodriguez, smiling wider than Hazel had ever seen him. "Is this some lesson about . . . like . . . reptiles?"

"I am not," Mr. Fernsby said, "talking about reptiles. I'm talking about creatures. About real-life monsters. *Them!* They don't have any other name. They probably did once, but they're incredibly old. Ancient. Even they, it's said, have forgotten what they were once called."

Hazel's neck grew hot. Beside her, Ava pursed her lips.

Around the class, the whispering started up again.

"I love Halloween," said Sheryl Jones from the back row.

"What kind of substitute is this?" asked Tarek Haddad.

"Do you think Ms. Jacobson knows about this?" said Miguel Rodriguez.

Hazel looked at Ava. "There's no such thing as monsters," she said.

She'd meant this only for Ava, but Mr. Fernsby must have heard because suddenly, he was staring at her. He took a few steps down her aisle.

Everyone fell silent.

Mr. Fernsby raised his eyebrows.

"No such thing as monsters?" he said. "Are you . . . certain?" He moved back to the front of the classroom, where he smoothed his suit and his tie. He ran his fingers through his beard once more.

A cold wave seemed to wash over the class.

"Best class ever," said Miguel Rodriguez. "Already, this is the best class ever."

Next to Hazel, Ava unpursed her lips. "Can you *please* just teach us about cells?" she said again.

But Tarek Haddad spoke. "Forget cells," he said. "I want to hear more about these monsters. What do they want?"

Other students nodded.

Hazel looked at Ava. *It's fine*, she mouthed.

"*Them*," Mr. Fernsby said, "want the same thing that every creature on Earth wants—to stay alive. For a long,

long time. Which *Them* do. They live on and on for thousands of years."

Hazel couldn't believe what she was hearing. In her own life science class.

"How?" Noah Haight asked. "How do they live for so long?"

Mr. Fernsby nodded.

"They touch you." He lifted a finger. "That's all. They touch you, and when they do, they drain away the life you have inside you." He began to walk back and forth across the front of the class. "Say, for example, that you are going to live for another fifty years. When one of *Them* looks at you, it knows this. It can see it. And if this . . . *thing* . . . touches you, it can steal away some of those years. Maybe ten. Maybe twenty. Maybe more. For *Them*, it's like drinking. They swallow your years up, and then they use those years for themselves. Your life gets shorter. And theirs gets longer. That's how they—how *Them*—are so old." Mr. Fernsby looked back at Noah Haight. "They've taken so many years from so many people for so very long."

Hazel turned to Ava again. Ava's eyes were closed as if this were a scary part in a movie. Hazel could practically hear her saying, *Tell me when it's over.*

From the back row, Sheryl Jones said, "What do *Them* look like?"

Mr. Fernsby raised a finger.

"An excellent question," he said. He took a few steps down Sheryl Jones's row. "*Them* look just like you and me, young lady. That's one reason they're such a mystery. We can't track *Them* down. We can't study *Them*. They blend in perfectly. They look like men, women, and children. There could be one in this classroom right now." He opened his arms wide. "And you would have no idea."

Everyone shifted and looked around as if they were checking for suspicious students among the rows of desks.

Hazel kept her eyes locked on Mr. Fernsby.

"Mostly, I've heard that *Them* like places where young people gather," he said. "Places where there is much life left to be lived. I've heard they spend their time in parks . . . or playgrounds . . . or schools."

Schools, Hazel thought.

"Can you please tell us about cells now?" Ava said, trying one more time to change the subject. She'd opened her eyes, but her voice came out quiet. "We have a test coming up."

Before Mr. Fernsby could answer, Tarek Haddad spoke.

"Tell us more," he said. "Tell us about how *Them* drink your years and use them for themselves."

"Ah," Mr. Fernsby said. "You want an example."

He walked up and down the aisles. His polished shoes made light tapping sounds on the tile floor. The furnace kicked on, and Hazel wondered what Mr. Fernsby would do next.

Then he stopped—Hazel couldn't believe it—right next to Ava's desk. He pointed at her.

"How old are you, young lady?" he said.

"Eleven," Ava said, and her voice came out barely louder than a whisper.

"Eleven," Mr. Fernsby repeated. "So young."

Hazel could see what Mr. Fernsby was doing. He was picking on Ava. Probably, she figured, he'd stopped at Ava's desk because she'd been the one who'd kept asking about cells. Or maybe, Hazel realized, he'd chosen Ava because he'd seen the way she'd been tapping her pencil and hunching her shoulders, and he knew he could get a reaction out of her.

"Let's imagine that you're going to live to be"—Mr. Fernsby studied Ava for a second—"ninety-one." He nodded. "That's eighty years of life you have left in you, young lady."

Ava didn't look up.

"Excuse me," Hazel said. "I also have a question about cells."

The substitute ignored her.

"When one of *Them* looks at you," he said, leaning down to Ava, "it knows you have these eighty years. It can see them. And to take them, all it has to do is touch you. Maybe it offers to shake your hand." He reached out a hand and let it hang over Ava's desk.

Ava shifted to the other side of her chair.

Tarek Haddad and Sheryl Jones in the back row chuckled.

Hazel glared at them.

"If you shake that hand"—Mr. Fernsby kept his hand hovering over Ava—"that's all it takes. You go still, and then this thing that looks just like you or me—the biggest mystery in all of life science—drinks some of your eighty years away."

"And you shrivel up like a raisin," Miguel Rodriguez said, and he laughed.

"No," Mr. Fernsby said, turning. "When one of *Them* is done with you, you look the same as you always did. Only, you have fewer years left. You're closer to . . . the end."

Hazel began kicking one of her desk's legs.

"Wait a minute," said Noah Haight. "You said they drink *some* of your years. They don't take all of them?"

"They do not," Mr. Fernsby said, turning back to Ava. His outstretched hand was still hovering over her. "They always leave you something. Maybe one year. Maybe two. Maybe ten. These creatures don't see themselves as murderers. Not really. They think they're just thieves, and what they steal is time."

Finally, Mr. Fernsby dropped his hand and walked back to the front of the class.

Hazel could hear Ava breathing quickly. She remembered the haunted corn maze from last year and the trembly look on Ava's face as she'd guided her out.

She had that same trembly look now.

Hazel narrowed her eyes.

"You're pretty good at making things up, Mr. Fernsby," said Tarek Haddad.

"Am I?" Mr. Fernsby said, raising his dark eyebrows. "Am I making things up?"

"Maybe he's not," said Mari Kuniyuki. She raised her cell phone. "He was right about the octopus. I looked it up. They do have three hearts. And he was right about snails too. They have thousands of teeth."

Mr. Fernsby didn't speak. He let the question of whether he was telling the truth hang in the air like his hand had hung over Ava.

In the next desk over, Ava put her head down.

There was nothing Hazel could do for her. She could ask about cells again, but everyone would ignore her.

The chance to change the subject was gone.

"You are of course free to make up your own minds about what I've told you today," Mr. Fernsby said. "You are free to doubt the life science lesson I have taught you. Or you are free to open your minds to a new possibility. The decision is yours."

"Hang on," said Miguel Rodriguez, and the smile he'd worn all class faded. "Is that what this is really about? A lesson about opening our minds?"

Mr. Fernsby combed his beard with his fingers.

"This has been a lesson about *Them,* young man," he said. "You can do with it what you want."

Slumped on her desk, Ava wasn't moving.

As far as Hazel could tell, Mr. Fernsby didn't even notice. He talked on and on, and the other students seemed to love it. They peppered him with questions.

What do people who are getting drained look like?

Do you know anyone who's ever met one of Them?

How many Them *are there in America right now?*

It went on for forty-five minutes. Finally, the bell rang. Everyone stood and began to shuffle out of the room. Everyone, that was, except for Ava and Hazel.

"Best substitute ever," said Noah Haight as he passed Hazel's desk.

"Halloween rules," said Sheryl Jones.

Ava still hadn't moved.

"Are you all right?" Hazel whispered.

Ava shrugged.

"It was only a story." Hazel touched Ava's shoulder. "It was a dumb Halloween lesson about opening our minds. You don't need to worry about it. I promise."

"I just don't like that feeling," Ava said. "The one I get when I hear those things."

"I know," Hazel said. "But you're safe. Trust me."

At the front of the class, Mr. Fernsby picked up his dusty book from Ms. Jacobson's desk. He started reading. He was probably getting ready for his performance in the next class.

Hazel could barely look at him. He'd made Ava slump and cower.

Somebody, she thought, *should do something.*

"I'm going to talk to him," Hazel said.

"Don't," Ava whispered. "He's just a stupid substitute."

"He picked on you," Hazel said. "He did it on purpose."

And that was true. But for Hazel, there was something else hanging in the air. Something else she needed to do.

"It'll only take a second," she said. "I'll meet you at lunch."

She pulled Ava up, and as Ava shuffled through the classroom door, Hazel checked to make sure she and Mr. Fernsby were really alone.

She walked to the front of the class. She flexed her fingers.

She didn't quite know how to start. She wanted to say something to Mr. Fernsby about what he had done. About how he'd picked on Ava and how afterward, he'd chosen not to notice her.

He was one of those adults—she'd seen so many of them—who think they're being funny when they're really being mean.

But she couldn't find the words to tell him this.

So instead, she walked up to Mr. Fernsby and asked him a question, one that had been on her mind all class.

"Where did you hear about *Them*, Mr. Fernsby?" she said. "Where did you learn it all?"

Without looking up, Mr. Fernsby waggled his book.

"I read a lot," he said. "I like old books. The ones most people have forgotten about."

Hazel nodded. She knew the books he meant.

"My friend Ava," she started to say, and then looked down.

She didn't know how to go on. Maybe it didn't matter. Some adults never learned anyway.

"I guess I just wanted to say thank you for the lesson, Mr. Fernsby," Hazel said. "And happy Halloween."

She reached out her hand.

Mr. Fernsby looked at it for a second. It must have seemed strange to him, Hazel realized, being offered a handshake by someone who was one-third his age.

Or someone who he thought was one-third his age.

Hazel smiled innocently.

You're a twelve-year-old girl, she told herself. *Just a twelve-year-old girl at school.*

And Mr. Fernsby must have believed that. Because despite his own story and all the old books he'd read, he smiled and said, "Happy Halloween to you too, young lady."

And he took Hazel's hand.

At once, she started drinking.

It was true, what Mr. Fernsby had said. *Them* weren't murderers. Just thieves. And Hazel had always been generous. She'd always left people at least ten years. Or fifteen. Usually more.

But as she drank, and as Mr. Fernsby's body went still and his mouth fell open, she remembered the way Ava had slumped in her desk, the way she'd closed her eyes at Mr. Fernsby's words, the way she'd become so silent and so afraid.

So afraid of . . . *Them*.

And so this time—for the first time—Hazel took everything.

The Perfect Girl

I T'S a stupid rule," Lucas said, stepping off the school bus. All day he'd been trying to get people to agree with him.

"I don't know," Cole answered, following him down the bus stairs. "It doesn't seem like that big of a deal to me."

Lucas shook his head. Cole could be so . . . *clueless*.

The rule was one Coach Gonzales had announced in gym class that morning. It had to do with the school Valentine's dance coming up in just one week.

"Since we'll be canceling gym on Valentine's Day to make time for the dance," Coach Gonzales had said after the boys had finished their warm-up calisthenics, "all students will be required to dance at least five songs. It will count as your physical activity for the day."

Lucas had groaned when Coach had said this.

"And you must share each of your five dances with a different partner," Coach went on.

Lucas had *really* groaned when Coach had said this.

The bus rumbled away, and Lucas and Cole began walking the two blocks to their homes.

"Shouldn't we get to choose whether we dance or not?" Lucas said. "Shouldn't that be up to us? And shouldn't we get to choose how many people we dance with?"

The boys turned onto Crestview Drive.

"It might not be that bad." Cole shrugged. "It might even make the dance more fun, you know? Getting people to dance instead of just leaning against the walls?"

"But five different partners?" Lucas said. "Who am I going to dance with?"

Next to him, Cole laughed. "Anyone," he said. "Dance with anyone."

Lucas rolled his eyes. *Clueless*, he thought. "You can't dance with just anyone at a Valentine's dance."

Cole raised his eyebrows. "Why not?"

"Because dancing is . . ." Lucas didn't know how to explain it. "Valentine's Day should be . . . It should be with someone you like. A lot."

"So dance with Hiromi Lin," Cole said. "You like her."

"I don't like her like *that*," Lucas said. "We're friends. Besides, she's way too tall. Dancing together, we'd look goofy."

"Well, what about Emily Rogers?"

"She's nice, I guess, but have you heard her laugh?" Lucas said. "It's like a foghorn. If I accidentally told a joke while we were dancing, my ears would ring for hours."

"Brittani Cook?"

"She plays the ukulele."

"What does that have to do with anything?" Cole said.

Lucas didn't answer. Cole, he decided, just wasn't getting it. *Clueless.*

Well, Lucas wasn't clueless. He knew about Valentine's dances, and he didn't want to spend his time dancing with just anyone. He wanted to spend it with a girl who was . . . *perfect*.

He thought through the girls in his classes.

Miley Armstrong? No. She spent too much time reading sappy romance novels.

Maya Jimenez? She painted her fingernails weird colors.

Abbi Hammari? She had wild hair.

He reached his house and climbed the three steps to his front porch.

"Why not just dance for fun?" Cole called from the sidewalk. "I mean, you're not exactly flawless either, you know."

Lucas turned and stared at Cole. Then, without answering, he stepped into his house and closed his front door.

Just dance for fun, he thought. He made a *pfft* sound.

He went into his kitchen to grab a snack. He pulled cheese, salami, and mustard out of the fridge and dumped them onto the counter.

That's when he saw her.

The Perfect Girl.

Her picture was sitting on top of a stack of mail piled up on the kitchen counter. It was in an ad for some clothing store Lucas had never heard of called Janson Trevor's.

He pushed his sandwich stuff aside and picked up the ad.

Whoa, he thought.

Because this girl really was perfect.

She had dark hair and dark eyes and smooth-looking skin. She wore red lipstick, a zipped black hoodie, and a red skirt. Her hair was curly and messy, but in just the right way, and she was leaning one shoulder against a graffiti-stained wall. She looked about thirteen—close to Lucas's age.

A flutter rose in his chest.

"Wow," he whispered.

Usually, the kids in clothing ads looked ridiculous, posed with fake smiles and perfectly combed hair. But there was something in this girl's eyes, a glance at the camera that said, *Yeah, I know. This is pretty silly, right?*

Lucas stared at her. He focused on the girl's cherry-red, half-puckered lips.

It felt like his chest was being pressed in from all sides. He held the ad gently, careful not to crinkle it.

He sat down at the kitchen table, forgetting about his sandwich.

This is who I want to dance with, he thought. Everything about this girl—her hair, her crooked smile, the look in her eyes—was perfect. He could tell she was smart. He could tell she was funny. He could tell she didn't play the ukulele or read too many sappy romance novels or laugh so loud she'd make your ears ring for hours.

A strange thought flickered in Lucas's head. Maybe he could write to Janson Trevor's and ask for this girl's name and email address. Maybe he could send her a message, and maybe, if he did, she'd write him back.

No. He shook himself.

He was being crazy.

This girl was a model in a clothing store ad, and he was Lucas Rawlins, a normal sixth grader at Canyons Middle School. He would never meet this girl.

Never.

The thought made him slump in his chair.

At least I have her picture, he thought. Slowly, he began tearing it out of the ad. He tore carefully. He didn't want to rip through the Perfect Girl. When he had her out, he folded the picture once, down the middle, and slid it into his back pocket.

He looked around to make sure his parents hadn't come home and seen him. He remembered the cheese and salami and mustard on the counter, but he stood and touched his pocket to make sure the Perfect Girl was still there.

Then he put all the food away without even making a sandwich.

⟨⟩

For the next few days, Lucas carried the Perfect Girl everywhere. Every time someone mentioned the Valentine's dance, he thought of her.

In his back pocket, she began to crinkle a little, but he kept her there anyway. He liked having her close.

When he thought no one was looking, he'd pull her out, unfold the picture, and look at her.

He especially liked the way her head was tilted in the picture, slightly toward the graffiti-stained wall. It was just right. Clever and quick and smart.

And he liked her lips.

Her cherry-red, half-puckered lips.

One day, he took her out and unfolded her under his desk while Mrs. Wallace was teaching everyone the properties of exponents. He looked at her for a long time without blinking, and suddenly, he wished he knew her name. He'd been thinking of her as the Perfect Girl for days, but now, he wanted her to have a *real* name. A *perfect* name.

He focused on her face and ran through a list of names in his head.

Riley. Olivia. Samantha.

He let out a little puff of air. No. Not good enough. Not for her.

Sophia. Bridget.

He puffed again. Not even close.

Diana. Bobbie. Valerie. Celeste.

He stopped.

Celeste.

Yes, he thought.

That was it.

That was her name. *Celeste.* It was pretty. Strong. Easy to say. And it was different. Unique, without being too weird.

"Celeste," he whispered, and in the picture, the Perfect Girl seemed to tilt her head a bit closer to the graffiti-stained wall and smile.

The day before the Valentine's dance, Lucas was looking at Celeste during free work time in Mr. Barton's chemistry class, when suddenly, a hand shot beneath his desk and snatched the picture away.

"What's this thing you're always looking at?" It was Cole. Clueless Cole.

"Hey," Lucas said. "That's mine." He tried to snatch the picture back, but Cole shifted. Lucas's face flushed. He didn't know how he was going to explain Celeste.

Cole squinted at the picture. "Who is this?"

Lucas shrugged.

"Wait a second," Cole said. "This is, like, magazine paper. Is this a picture from a magazine?"

Lucas didn't speak.

"Seriously," Cole said. He waved the picture. "I've seen you looking at this all the time. What's up?"

"That girl is . . ." Lucas said. "She's . . ."

He tried to think of something to say.

"What?" Cole said. "What is she?"

"She's the reason I don't want to follow Coach Gonzales's stupid rules at the Valentine's dance tomorrow," Lucas said. "She's . . . my girlfriend."

Just like that, the words were out. *My girlfriend.*

"No way," Cole said. He shook his head. "Your girl-friend?" Cole held up the picture. "This is your girlfriend?"

Lucas gave a half nod.

"So why's this picture on magazine paper?" Cole said, his voice dripping with doubt. "You obviously ripped it out of something." Cole fingered the torn edges.

"It's from an ad," Lucas said, finally snatching it back. "From a store called Janson Trevor's."

Cole raised his eyebrows.

"Celeste is . . . kind of a model."

"Celeste?" Cole said.

Lucas folded the picture and slid it back into his pocket.

"No way." Cole stared at him.

Lucas didn't answer.

Cole pointed to Lucas's pocket and scowled. "If that's your girlfriend, where'd you meet her?"

Lucas could tell this was a test. He tried to answer naturally.

"We met two months ago at the mall in front of Juicy Straws."

Cole stared at him. "What was she wearing?"

"Ripped jeans and a black jacket," Lucas answered.

Cole shook his head again. "Let me see the picture," he said.

Slowly, Lucas slid Celeste out of his pocket and passed her over.

Cole squinted. Lucas could tell he was starting to consider it.

Clueless Cole, he thought.

"What's her favorite food?" Cole asked.

"Peanut butter," Lucas said. It was a dumb answer, he knew, but he tried not to flinch.

"When's her birthday?"

"August third."

"What kind of music does she like?"

"She calls it indie-pop."

"Where does she go to school?"

"East Jordan across town, but she hates it and wants to transfer here."

His answers came surprisingly easy, but he'd spent so much time thinking about Celeste—wondering about her—that he didn't feel like he was lying to Cole as much as he was sharing details that were already in his head, that already felt true.

"Have you held her hand?" Cole said.

"Uh, well, yeah," Lucas said, trying to sound casual. "She *is* my girlfriend."

Cole leaned forward and lowered his voice.

"Have you kissed her?"

Lucas paused. He wasn't sure how to answer this one. The truth was, he'd thought about what it might be like to kiss Celeste. He'd never kissed a girl before, but how could he not think about it when her head was tilted and her cherry-red, half-puckered lips were always turned up . . . toward him.

But he'd nearly convinced Cole. He could tell. His answer to this one question might, he knew, settle things for good. If Lucas said he had kissed the Perfect Girl, Cole might never believe him. It would be too much to swallow. But if Lucas said he hadn't kissed her . . .

Lucas sat up. He looked Cole in the eyes.

"We haven't kissed," he said. "Not yet."

Cole raised an eyebrow.

"We're waiting for the right moment," Lucas said.

The right moment.

Lucas pictured meeting Celeste in real life. He pictured leaning close to her, closing his eyes, and actually . . .

He shook his head.

"Well, I'll be," Cole said. He passed Celeste back to Lucas. "You actually have a girlfriend! And she's a model!" Cole folded his arms. "Why didn't you tell me?"

⌐◦⌐

Clueless Cole, it turned out, had a pretty big mouth. By the next morning, Valentine's Day, everyone knew about Lucas's girlfriend. His *model* girlfriend.

Braxton Moore, a football player who'd never even talked to Lucas, high-fived him in the hallway as Lucas came in the main entrance. A few seconds later, Luis Perez—an eighth grader who called all sixth graders untouchables—sidled up to Lucas in the hallway and asked if he could see the picture Lucas kept in his pocket.

As he walked to class, all around him, people whispered, conversations stopped, and students' heads turned.

Blood rushed to Lucas's face.

This isn't what I wanted, he thought as he sat down in Mrs. Wallace's algebra class. *This isn't what I wanted at all.*

He knew what to do, though. He'd let it go on for a couple of weeks—the rumors, the questions, the head turns—and he'd start keeping her picture in his top dresser drawer at home. Before long, everyone would forget about Celeste. This was middle school, after all. Gossip swirled up, buzzed in the air, and died away. His classmates would probably forget about Celeste in just a few hours when the Valentine's dance fired up all kinds of new things to talk about.

The Valentine's dance, Lucas thought. What was he going to do about it?

The bell rang. Mrs. Wallace started speaking.

"Class," she said. "Before we begin, I'd like to introduce a new student who's just joined us. She's transferred here from East Jordan across town."

Lucas looked up from his notebook.

Standing beside Mrs. Wallace was . . .

No, Lucas thought. *It can't be*. But it was. He'd looked at her picture a thousand times. He knew her skin, her eyes, her hair. It was definitely her.

Celeste.

She was wearing the same clothes as in the ad—the red skirt, the black hoodie. She was even wearing the cherry-red lipstick.

Lucas's chest closed in. It was the Perfect Girl. Right in his classroom. He couldn't believe it. He'd be able to meet her and talk to her and learn her real name and maybe even do a science project with her and one day . . .

Oh, no. He shuddered. *Her real name.*

Clueless Cole had seen the picture of Celeste. He knew what she looked like. He was sitting right behind Lucas, and he was about to learn the truth—that Lucas really had just ripped a picture from the Janson Trevor's ad and given "Celeste" a made-up name and life.

In a few seconds, Mrs. Wallace would tell everyone the Perfect Girl's real name, and then Cole—big-mouthed Cole—would know.

Everyone would know.

"I'd like you to give a warm welcome to . . ." Mrs. Wallace said, and time seemed to slow down. Lucas felt blood rush to his ears. ". . . our newest classmate . . . Celeste."

Lucas shook himself. *Celeste?* Had Mrs. Wallace just said the Perfect Girl's name was *Celeste?* He turned to Cole.

Cole stared back. His mouth gaped. "Your girlfriend!" he whispered.

"I want you all to be especially nice to Celeste today," Mrs. Wallace went on. "It can be hard, transferring to a school full of strangers. Especially on Valentine's Day."

Celeste spoke, her voice smooth and slow.

"Oh, I'm not in a school full of strangers," she said. She tossed her head, flipping her perfectly curly, perfectly messy hair. "I know Lucas." She pointed at him.

Everyone turned.

"Lucas and I are . . . really good friends."

And the way she said *really good friends*, kind of lilting and with a half giggle at the end, made Lucas's stomach tingle.

"If it's all right with you, Mrs. Wallace," Celeste said, "I'll take the seat next to him."

Then she walked down the row and slid into the empty desk beside him.

"Hi, Lucas," she said slowly. She smiled and tucked a loose strand of messy black hair behind one ear.

"Well," Mrs. Wallace said. "Isn't that nice."

⌁

Lucas's mind raced.

How was this happening?

She was the Perfect Girl. And her name really was Celeste. And somehow, she knew him. She knew his name. And she'd told everyone they were "really good friends."

But he'd never met her.

Not in real life, anyway.

Now she was sitting in the next desk over, staring at him.

All through algebra, she did nothing else.

When Mrs. Wallace explained how to factor trinomials, she *stared at him*. When Cole tapped Celeste's desk and introduced himself, she *stared at him*. Even when Darrin Whiteside fumbled with the pencil sharpener at the back of the room and spilled pencil shavings everywhere, she *stared at him*. The whole time, she sat sideways in her desk, her eyes fixed on him, her head tilted, her lips half puckered.

Finally, the bell rang, and Lucas stood. Celeste stood too. He walked slowly toward the classroom door, and so did Celeste, matching him step for step. He pushed into the crowded hallway, and she stayed next to him, not even two feet away.

Then, as if she'd done it a thousand times, she reached down and took his hand.

And held it.

The air in the hallway grew thick.

People nudged each other and whispered.

"Lucas's girlfriend," he heard someone say.

He felt sweat beading on his forehead.

"This'll be so great," Celeste said as they walked down the hallway, her voice still smooth and slow. "You and me, at the same school."

She looked at him. She seemed so comfortable. Her hand was cool and dry, not clammy and wet like his.

There was a part of him that wanted to enjoy this. After all, this was the Perfect Girl, and she was holding his hand! She was wearing her red skirt and her black hoodie and her cherry-red lipstick! And she was calling herself his *girlfriend*!

But his heart would not stop pounding. Who was this girl? How did she know him? And how was her name Celeste?

They came to a bottleneck of people next to a drinking fountain. Lucas shifted sideways, and Celeste squeezed his hand tighter.

She rubbed her thumb over one of his knuckles.

Goose bumps rose on his arms.

"Can you bring peanut butter into the cafeteria here?" Celeste said as they kept walking. "At my last school, you couldn't. There was this kid who was super allergic to peanuts. If he even touched a peanut, he'd swell up and maybe even die. It was too bad, because peanut butter is my favorite food." She squeezed his hand again. "But you already knew that, didn't you?"

Something seemed to ripple across Lucas's skin.

He needed a minute—a minute to think without her right next to him, holding his hand—so he said, "I'll be right back," and he ducked into the boys' bathroom.

He leaned over a sink.

"She's real," he whispered. "She's actually real."

He wasn't sure what he should be feeling. Fear? Wonder? Joy?

He closed his eyes. In his mind, her perfectly tilted head and her cherry-red lips flashed.

He reached into his back pocket and pulled out her picture. He unfolded it.

There, like always, were the alley and the graffiti-stained wall, but where Celeste had been standing before, there was no one. The picture was just a wall and an empty alley.

With no Celeste.

Lucas opened his mouth, but no sounds came out.

She's real, he thought. But she wasn't *just* real.

She was also *out*.

— ~ —

She sat by him in every class that day . . . just staring.

The Perfect Girl, he kept thinking, and little by little, he remembered that her eyes really did look quick and clever, that her hair really was curly and messy in just the right way, and that her cherry-red lips really were full and red and . . . perfect.

So as he walked with Celeste out of Mr. Barton's chemistry class, he did something.

He held his breath and took her hand.

He did it before she even had the chance to take his. When he did it, he looked at her, and she smiled.

Finally, classes ended, and Principal Khan's voice rang out over the PA system. All students, he said, were to make their way to the gym for the Valentine's dance.

A minute later, Lucas and Celeste walked into the gym hand in hand.

A disco ball hung from the ceiling. Music blared. Red and white streamers trailed down from the basketball hoops. A few kids walked to the center of the basketball court, and Lucas saw Cole dancing with Hiromi Lin.

"Five dances!" Coach Gonzales called out from in front of the bleachers. "That's the assignment! I'm keeping track." He tapped a clipboard.

Lucas and Celeste stood to the side. They didn't speak. After a few minutes, a slow song started and Celeste pulled Lucas to the middle of the dance floor. She put her arms around his neck and began swaying from side to side.

"Lucas," she said, her voice soft, "I need to ask you something."

Lucas nodded.

"Why haven't we kissed yet?" she said, and she tilted her head.

The floor beneath him seemed to shift.

"We've been dating for two months," she said, "since we met at the mall, in front of Juicy Straws, remember?"

She inched closer. He could feel heat coming from her lips.

"We were waiting," Lucas said, stumbling over his words, "for the right moment."

"It's Valentine's Day," she said. "And we're dancing."

Lucas swallowed.

He'd imagined this moment. He'd thought about it again and again. Now, impossibly, it was here.

Could he do it?

She's the Perfect Girl, he told himself.

Whoever she was, wherever she'd come from, he knew her better than anyone, didn't he? He knew her name and her birthday and her favorite food and what she'd been wearing the day they'd met. And he knew so much more. He knew she didn't play the ukulele or laugh too loud or read sappy romance novels. He knew everything there was to know about her, he figured, because he'd given her these things, hadn't he? He'd spoken them and made them true.

So one kiss would be fine, he told himself.

He leaned forward. The music around him faded.

He tilted his head. He closed his eyes.

My first kiss, he thought.

And then his lips touched hers.

Her lips were soft and warm and slightly sticky with lipstick. At once, everything in his head turned cloudy and white.

The music faded out completely. He thought maybe he should put his hands on Celeste's face, like people did on TV.

But he seemed to have become paralyzed. Completely frozen.

The kiss went on, though Lucas couldn't tell how long it

lasted. One second? Ten? Twenty? And then Celeste pulled away.

It was over.

Lucas felt warm, but he still didn't move. His mind cleared. He opened his eyes.

Where was Celeste?

She wasn't in front of him anymore.

And the music from the dance was gone.

What had happened?

He tried to turn his head, but he couldn't. He tried to take a step back, but his feet seemed cemented to the floor. Suddenly, he didn't know where he was. Everything around him—the lighting, the ground below his feet, the air—felt different.

He tried to call Celeste's name.

He couldn't even move his mouth.

All he could see was an alley in front of him and a graffiti-stained wall to his side.

Nothing seemed to be working. Not his hands, not his legs, not his neck. He couldn't even blink.

Then he figured it out. He knew where he was. The alley and the graffiti-stained wall. He'd carried them in his pocket. He'd seen them a thousand times.

Now, as he struggled to move but couldn't, they were the only things he could see.

They were the only things he would ever see.

LUMPY, LUMPY

THE thing about oatmeal is . . . I hate it. And I don't just hate it a little bit. I hate it with all the force of a thousand exploding suns. When I have to put even one spoonful into my mouth, I gag.

Seriously.

I retch, and the back of my tongue comes up. I have to fight just to keep from puking everywhere.

It's the texture.

Lumpy, lumpy.

Like eating mud. Or paste. Or cow droppings.

I know what you're thinking. Have I tried it with brown sugar? Strawberries and cream? Chocolate chips? Coconut flakes?

Well, the answers are *yes*, *yes*, *yes*, and *yes*.

I've tried oatmeal every which way you can make it, and I don't care what's added to it. It's still gloopy and gross.

I mean, if you told me to eat a spare tire and then sprinkled it with chocolate chips, would that make the spare tire any more delicious? Of course not. It would still be a spare tire. It would still be disgusting and inedible. Just like oatmeal.

So when I sat down at my spot at the breakfast bar one

morning and Mom slid my favorite yellow bowl in front of me, I kind of couldn't believe it.

Because it was filled to the brim with—you guessed it—oatmeal. Colorless, clumpy oatmeal.

"Hey," I said, "this is—"

But Mom interrupted me.

"Yeah, Elena," she said. "Deal with it."

"But—" I said, and before I could go on, Mom scooped up a handful of blueberries from a bowl on the counter and dropped three of them into my favorite yellow bowl. She popped the rest into her mouth.

"Try it with blueberries," she said, munching, not understanding the whole spare-tire-chocolate-chip thing. "Just eat it, Elena. You can't live on cold cereal forever."

Mom thinks I'm a "picky eater." But is it "picky" to not want lumpy globs of goo shifting around in your mouth? Is it "picky" to think food should be something you have to actually chew before you swallow?

"Besides," she said, "I can't afford to throw away any more food, Elena. I just spent two hundred dollars on that." She pointed to where our new microwave hung over the stove. Our old microwave had stopped working, so Mom had saved for weeks to buy this one and spent an entire Saturday afternoon installing it. "So let's be smart and stop throwing food away, okay?"

"Fine," I said, and I picked up a spoon.

But don't think for a second that I ate any of that putrid oatmeal. While Mom fussed around the kitchen, I stirred it and poked at it and tried not to smell it. As soon as Mom walked down the hall, I jumped up and scraped it into the garbage. Then I shifted the trash around so the dumped oatmeal would be hidden under a crumpled piece of plastic wrap, a gum wrapper, and an old rubber band.

Quickly, before Mom came back into the kitchen, I swiped two granola bars out of the pantry and tucked them into my backpack. I planned to eat them on the bus to school so I wouldn't starve to death.

And I thought that'd be the end of it.

It should have been too.

But that night, long after Mom and I had gone to bed, something happened.

I woke up because I heard something. It was a kind of *whirr* or *buzz*. My room is the first one down the hallway, and the *whirr* was coming from the main living area. I could tell.

I checked the clock by my bed.

It said 3:13. What could be whirring and buzzing at 3:13 in the morning?

I stood up and stumbled, groggy, into the hall.

The house was completely dark except for a strange blue light glowing from the kitchen. When I got closer, I could see that it was the new microwave. It was on. And there was something inside it, spinning slowly.

"Mom?" I said. I figured she was making a late-night snack.

She didn't answer. I checked for her in the chairs at the table and at the breakfast bar. It didn't seem like she was in any of them. There was no movement. No dark shadows.

The microwave kept whirring. The blue light shifted as whatever was inside kept on spinning.

It was eerie, the house dark except for this one microwave light. The whole kitchen seemed to be bathed in a strange radioactive glow.

"Mom?" I said again.

Nothing.

The microwave counted down.

Seven . . . six . . . five.

What was happening? Was the microwave malfunctioning already? Coming on in the middle of the night all by itself? We'd only had the thing three days.

The countdown hit two . . . then one . . . and the microwave dinged. Its inside light went off and the kitchen went pitch-dark, except for the microwave's screen, which said End.

I switched on a light and squinted against the sudden brightness. Then I opened the microwave door.

There was my favorite yellow bowl.

It was filled to the brim with . . . oatmeal.

Steam rose up from it. I lifted the bowl out, slowly, and the sides of it almost burned my fingers.

"What on earth?" I said.

The oatmeal had blueberries in it. Three of them.

Weird, I thought. *Too weird.*

"Hello?" I whispered.

No one answered. I looked around.

This had to be Mom. She must have found my dumped oatmeal and decided to teach me a lesson.

"Okay, Mom," I said. "I get it. I'm not supposed to waste food. I'm sorry."

I waited for her to answer, to step out of the pantry and laugh.

She didn't.

Then I noticed something.

There weren't just three blueberries and oatmeal in my favorite yellow bowl. There was other stuff—a crumpled piece of plastic wrap, a gum wrapper, and even a thin rubber band.

It was like this was the same oatmeal I'd dumped that morning, like someone had scooped it right out of the garbage and caught up bits of trash with it.

The hair on my arms prickled. Quickly, I dumped the oatmeal into the trash again.

Then I put my yellow bowl in the sink, switched off the light, and practically ran back to bed.

Mom didn't say anything about the oatmeal the next morning. She even let me eat cereal for breakfast—Yo-Ho-Ohs, with pirate treasure marshmallows. My favorite.

I figured she thought I'd learned my lesson and everything was fine.

Then night came.

For the second night in a row, a *whirr*, or a muffled *buzz*, woke me up. I opened my eyes and checked my clock.

It was 3:13 a.m.

I stumbled out of bed, and it was like déjà vu. There was the eerie blue light coming from the microwave, and there was the spinning bowl inside. There was the countdown, three . . . two . . . one, and the *ding*, and the green glowing word.

End.

Then there was me, lifting out my favorite yellow bowl. It was filled with steaming oatmeal—again—and three blueberries. Mixed in, there was a gum wrapper, a crumpled piece of plastic wrap, a thin rubber band, and now, a paper clip and a bit of orange peel.

Once more, I scraped it all into the trash.

"I get it, Mom," I said. "Point made. I won't waste food."

She had to be hiding in the pantry. I threw the door open.

She wasn't there.

I checked in the coat closet and under the computer desk.

She wasn't anywhere.

Shivering a little, I shuffled down the hall. At the door to Mom's room, I turned the doorknob and peered in.

She was curled up in bed, eyes closed, hands tucked in front of her. She wasn't snoring exactly, but her breathing was heavy and regular, as if she'd been asleep for a long time.

A lump rose in my throat.

Before I could think too hard about things, I darted through the house, turning off lights.

I slid into bed, pulling the covers all the way over my head.

— ∼ —

It happened the next night. And the next night. And the night after that.

At the exact same time.

3:13 a.m.

I tried to ignore the microwave and sleep through the *whirr* and *buzz*, or at least stay in bed at 3:13 a.m., but I couldn't. The microwave seemed to have some strange power. The *whirr* was like music, calling to me. Like the Pied Piper.

Within a week, bags had formed under my eyes.

I kind of stopped sleeping at night. My head drooped in school, a lot, and I even fell asleep in math class.

One night, I decided to throw away the oatmeal somewhere other than the garbage, somewhere it'd be hard to find. So when I lifted out my favorite yellow bowl, I carried it to the back door. Even though it was cold outside, I slid the door open, stumbled into the bushes by the side of the house, and scraped the garbage-y oatmeal into the dirt by our hydrangea bush.

It didn't work.

The next night, at 3:13 a.m., I woke to the sound of a *whirr*. The oatmeal was back in the microwave, back in my favorite yellow bowl. Now it held three blueberries, a gum wrapper, a crumpled piece of plastic wrap, a paper clip, a bit of orange peel, a few dirt clods, a weedy-looking leaf, and a dead black beetle.

— ⁓ —

It kept going. I stopped sleeping altogether. I would just lie awake, in bed, waiting for what I knew would come.

Whirr. Buzz. Ding.

End.

In the mornings, I'd stumble into the bathroom, groggy. Before showering, I'd sit at the edge of the tub with my head in my hands.

I started napping during lunch. I found a quiet spot in the library between two bookshelves, and I used my backpack as a pillow.

More and more junk kept getting mixed in with the oatmeal. A sucker stick. An apple stem. A used, crumpled Band-Aid.

After two more weeks, a crust formed on top of the oatmeal, and then bits of mold appeared. They were small spots at first, but they grew a bit bigger each night.

Here's a question for you:

Do you know what it's like to be haunted? By a microwave?

I'll bet you don't.

I'm probably the only person in the whole long history of the world who understands what it's like to be called out of bed each night—each and every night—by a whirring microwave and have a bowl of oatmeal—the exact same bowl of oatmeal—shoved in your face again and again as it slowly grows dirtier and grosser and moldier.

After more than a month, my eyes ached with exhaustion. Red veins spiderwebbed through them. I started falling asleep in the strangest places—at a restaurant, in the dentist's chair, on the bus.

"What's up with you, Elena?" Mom asked one night at the dinner table. "You seem so tired. It doesn't make any sense."

"I'm just not sleeping well," I told her. "That's all."

Then one night, I stumbled out into the strange blue light, and my arms felt heavy. So heavy. When the microwave dinged and my favorite yellow bowl stopped spinning, I knew it was time to do something.

Unless I did, this would keep happening every night for the rest of my life, at exactly 3:13 a.m. I would keep growing more and more tired as the whirring, buzzing microwave kept returning my nasty, steaming, putrid bowl of oatmeal, which would be, each night, a little bit smellier, a little bit dirtier, a little bit nastier.

It was time to eat.

I knew that was the deal.

I had to eat it to end it.

This oatmeal wasn't going to get any better with time. Those mold spots weren't going to start shrinking. And that crust on top wasn't going to go soft. The mixed-in dirt and Band-Aid and dead beetle weren't going to disappear.

If I kept dumping it, the oatmeal would just keep getting nastier and nastier. It would turn completely green and fuzzy, and it would start to seep and smell like the bottom of our garbage bin.

If I didn't do something soon, it might even become infested with maggots.

It was time.

Eat it, I thought. *Eat it and end it.*

I reached into the microwave and lifted out my yellow bowl, which, I realized, wasn't my favorite anymore. Slowly, I pulled a spoon from the drawer. I caught a whiff of the oatmeal then, like a sewer drain, and I gagged. I flicked on the kitchen light and immediately wished I hadn't, because I saw everything that had piled up in the oatmeal—the gum wrapper, the dirt, the beetle, the rubber band, the paper clip, the plastic wrap, the Band-Aid, the orange peel, the sucker stick, the wilted weed, and the spots of mold, which were now the size of quarters.

But I was tired.

Can you understand that?

I was so, so tired.

So I took my place at the kitchen table. I held my breath and plugged my nose. I gripped my spoon.

I counted to three.

And I ate.

Hi, Jenny.

JENNY'S cell phone buzzed during the worst part of English class—Personal Reading Time, or PRT. During PRT, you weren't supposed to talk to your neighbor or doodle in your notebook or even ask to go to the bathroom. You were just supposed to sit there with a book.

Her cell phone was in her back pocket, and when it went off, its buzz tickled. Jenny smiled at the tickle, but she tamped her smile down quickly.

Technically, she wasn't supposed to have her cell phone.

"There should be absolutely no cell phone use during PRT!" Mrs. Evergarten always said. "Cell phones are the plague of your generation."

Jenny rolled her eyes whenever Mrs. Evergarten said this.

The plague of our generation? Please.

She checked Mrs. Evergarten at the front of the classroom. The gray-haired teacher was grading an essay, staring at a typed page with a half scowl on her face and a waggling red pen in her hand. Slowly, Jenny eased her phone out of her pocket.

Since getting it a month ago, she'd been trying to come up with the perfect name for her phone, something catchy.

She'd called her phone all sorts of things—Gizmo, Widget, Knickknack.

But nothing had really stuck.

As she eased her phone under her desk, though, an idea hit her.

She had it.

The perfect cell phone name.

Buzz-buzz.

Because that's what her phone gave her whenever it went off—two buzzes. One as it vibrated and another inside her chest. Some days, right when she woke up, she'd text every single one of her contacts a simple *hi* just so she could spend the whole morning getting their responses. Getting a jolt, a lift . . . a *buzz-buzz.*

Before clicking her phone, she checked Mrs. Evergarten at the front of the classroom one more time.

If she got caught using Buzz-buzz—she smiled at the name—her phone would be confiscated and sent to the main office, where it would be held until the end of the day.

This had happened to Jenny four times already.

At the front of the room, though, Mrs. Evergarten was scowling and scribbling a red-penned comment on the essay she'd been reading.

She'll never notice, Jenny thought. *I'll just check real quick under my desk.*

She pressed the button that brought Buzz-buzz to life and read the new text.

Hi, Jenny.

That was all it said. It was from a number she didn't recognize.

She made a face. She'd hoped the text would be from her best friend, Sophie Wynn, or from her field hockey teammate Aaliyah Haddad, or maybe even from Zach Wilcox—the perfectly-tanned-gorgeously-haired Zach Wilcox—who was sitting at a desk just across the room. She turned her head, but Zach was reading, no cell phone in sight.

Jenny sighed.

She peered at her phone again.

Hi, Jenny.

Something about the text felt . . . off.

It was the punctuation, she decided. It looked wrong. A comma after *Hi*? A period after *Jenny*? No one did that. Plus, the text had two capital letters, an *H* and a *J*, both in the right places.

Weird, she thought.

She started typing out her usual reply to numbers she didn't recognize:

new phone who dis :)

Before she finished, Mrs. Evergarten stood up at the front of the room. Quickly, Jenny tucked Buzz-buzz under one leg. She grabbed the book she was supposed to be reading—*Brave New World*—and leaned in, faking interest.

Slowly, Mrs. Evergarten walked up and down the aisles, glancing at the students' books. She commented on a few of them, and after a minute, she returned to the front of the classroom. She picked up another essay and her red pen.

Jenny lowered her book.

Her phone buzzed again. Wedged between her leg and her chair, the phone made her jump. She inched Buzz-buzz out from under her leg.

The new text was from the same mystery number. It said:

> That was a close one, Jenny. Mrs. Evergarten almost caught you.

Jenny's neck hairs tingled.

She looked around. Whoever was texting her had to be someone who could see her, someone in the classroom. She checked Zach again. He was still reading.

Up and down the rows, everyone—Lucía Flores, Jefferson Rigby, Tracy Bingham—seemed to be reading their books, following the super-dumb rules of PRT.

Who could it be? Jenny thought.

Buzz.

She looked down.

It's me, Jenny. It's Buzz-buzz.

Jenny startled and dropped her phone.

It clattered to the floor, and Mrs. Evergarten looked up.

What had just happened?

"Jenny McCloud," Mrs. Evergarten said. She made a *tsk, tsk* sound with her mouth. "Is that your cell phone on the floor? Were you using it during Personal Reading Time . . . again?"

Jenny didn't answer. A few students snickered.

Jenny bent and picked up her phone. She had *just* named it, not two minutes earlier. How could someone already be texting her pretending to be Buzz-buzz?

"Bring it to me." Mrs. Evergarten held out her hand. "You know the rules. You can collect it from the main office at the end of the day."

Jenny stood and walked slowly. Her phone felt hot.

She paused before passing Buzz-buzz to Mrs. Evergarten. She wanted to take one more look at the texts, to make sure she'd really seen them right, but Mrs. Evergarten cleared her throat.

"The plague of your generation," she said. She took the phone between two fingers and dropped it, not gently, into her top desk drawer.

Jenny shuffled back to her seat, ignoring the smirks and grins of her classmates. She glanced at Zach Wilcox again. He hadn't even looked up from his book.

She felt her face go pink.

She pictured the last message she'd received.

It's me, Jenny. It's Buzz-buzz.

— ❧ —

When the final bell rang, Jenny bolted for the main office. How many texts, she wondered, had she missed in the last three hours?

All day, she'd been searching for an explanation for the strange texts she'd received during PRT, and she'd finally found one. She must have been whispering to herself while she'd been sitting in English class. Her mom did that sometimes—whispered to herself without realizing it—especially when she was driving or wasting time on her computer. Maybe Jenny had picked up the habit?

Somebody in Mrs. Evergarten's class *must* have heard her and decided to make a big joke out of it. It was probably Jaxon Hamilton. He sat right in front of Jenny, and this was the kind of thing he'd think was hilarious.

Of course my own phone isn't texting me, Jenny thought.

Still, all day, pictures of the carefully punctuated text messages kept worming their way back into Jenny's mind.

Hi, Jenny.

That was a close one, Jenny. Mrs. Evergarten
almost caught you.

It's me, Jenny. It's Buzz-buzz.

She shook her head.

Ha ha, Jaxon. Very funny.

She pulled open the main office doors. The secretary,
Mr. Hawkins, shot her a grin.

"Jenny McCloud," he said, shaking his head. "Mrs.
Evergarten said you'd be making an appearance here
today." He reached for a shoebox that was sitting on
his desk. The box had black stripes on it that were
meant to look like iron bars. The words ALCATRAZ: AN
INESCAPABLE PRISON FOR CRIMINAL PHONES had been
scrawled across its side. Mr. Hawkins lifted the lid and
pulled Buzz-buzz out of it.

"Has it . . . um . . . been going off a lot?" Jenny asked.

"I haven't been paying attention," Mr. Hawkins said. "I
do have a job, you know." He waved a hand around the
main office, as if this showed how busy he was. "Some of us
have things to do besides goof off on our phones."

He smirked as Jenny took Buzz-buzz. The second she did,
the phone vibrated.

She walked quickly out of the office and looked down.

Hi, Jenny.

There it was again. The same text, with the capital letters and the correct punctuation. The phone buzzed again.

> I don't like it in Alcatraz, Jenny. Please don't
> get me sent there anymore.

Jenny stopped walking.

Where are you, Jaxon Hamilton? she thought. He had to be watching her from somewhere.

She turned a full circle, but the school halls were nearly empty. A lone sixth grader scuttled past carrying a trumpet case.

Another buzz.

> This isn't Jaxon, Jenny. I told you. It's me.
> It's Buzz-buzz.

Jenny brought her hand to her mouth. A shiver ran down her spine.

Had she been whispering to herself? In the hallway? She didn't think so. Besides, there was no one around to hear.

Just then, Zach Wilcox came around a corner in his basketball uniform. Jenny tried to put the strange texts out of her mind. She smoothed her hair.

Buzz. She glanced at her phone.

Talk to Zach, Jenny. This is your chance.

Jenny's eyes darted up and down the hallway.

Who is this?

She had no idea. And she had no idea how they knew about Zach . . . or the name Buzz-buzz. But she didn't think this was funny. Not one bit.

Zach came closer. Jenny stood up straight and tried to smile. She rested a hand on her hip.

Her phone buzzed again.

Would you like me to search the internet for
conversation starters?

Leave me alone, Jenny thought. She folded her arms and pressed Buzz-buzz against her ribs. Her whole face felt tight. Zach came closer, closer, and then he passed.

She didn't even say hi.

Nice going, she thought. *Really smooth.*

Buzz.

She checked her phone.

Don't worry, Jenny. You'll get another chance.
I'll make sure of it.

Who? She looked up and down the halls. *How?*

It didn't matter, she told herself. She knew just what to do. Her mom had prepared her for this exact thing on the day she'd gotten her phone.

"If anyone ever sends you texts that make you feel uncomfortable," she'd said, "block their number, okay? You don't respond, and you don't engage. You block them."

Jenny stepped to the side of the hallway. On her phone screen, she touched the word *Edit* next to the mystery number.

The phone buzzed.

What are you doing, Jenny?

She scrolled and pointed at the words *Block This Number*.
Buzz.

Please wait.

She lowered her finger.
Buzz. Buzz. Buzz.

Jenny.

No.

Stop.

Quickly, she touched her finger to the screen.

Number Blocked, her cell phone said. Jenny waited. Buzz-buzz stayed quiet. She looked around.

Good riddance, she thought. Her heart slowed. Her muscles settled. Now she could get back to normal. She could read the texts she'd missed while her phone had been locked up in Alcatraz.

She checked and there were twenty-seven of them.

Twenty-seven new texts, she thought, and the familiar buzz swelled in her chest. As she left the school, she scrolled though her messages and sent her best friend, Sophie Wynn, a meme about book reports. She sent her field hockey teammate Aaliyah Haddad a video from their last match.

Halfway home, her phone buzzed.

Hi, Jenny.

She stopped in the middle of the sidewalk.

A comma. A period. A capital *H* and *J*.

The phone buzzed again.

Blocking me wasn't very nice.

Buzz.

Not very nice at all.

She blocked that number.

And she blocked the number that texted her after that.

And the number after that.

But it didn't matter. The texts kept coming. They rolled in, one after another, like pounding waves.

At home, in her bedroom, she lost track of how many numbers she'd blocked. She'd fallen into a pattern.

Buzz.

Hi, Jenny.

Block.

Buzz.

Hi, Jenny.

Block.

Then, as she sat on her bed, wondering when the mystery texter would finally give up, the pattern changed.

Buzz.

Please, Jenny.

Block.

Buzz.

Text me back, Jenny.

Block.

Buzz.

I'll tell everyone your secret, Jenny.

Jenny stopped.

She squeezed Buzz-buzz in her hands.

Zach, she thought.

Buzz.

Yes. Zach.

Buzz.

You have 107 contacts, Jenny. Did you know that?

Jenny put her phone down. She backed away from it.

What do you want? she thought.

Buzz.

She leaned forward.

I want you to text me back.

Buzz.

I'm like you, Jenny. I like getting texts. I like the way they make me feel.

Buzz-buzz, she thought.

Her phone vibrated.

Yes. Buzz-buzz.

She backed away from her phone even farther.

How could this be happening?

If Buzz-buzz really was texting her, how did her phone know what she was thinking? How was it reading her mind? Could phones do that? And how could a phone—a machine made of plastic and metal—be thinking for itself, texting for itself?

She turned her head. There was no one in her room. Her blinds were closed.

Could this really be Buzz-buzz?

Buzz.

She leaned forward.

Yes, Jenny. It's me.

She reached for her phone. *Please leave me alone*, she thought.

Buzz.

No, Jenny.

Buzz.

That's not what I do.

Buzz.

Text me or I'll tell everyone your secret.

Jenny's fingers trembled. Still, she started typing out a text. For some reason, she punctuated it and capitalized it correctly. Her text said:

Hi, Buzz-buzz. What's up?

She hit *Send*.

———

Buzz-buzz was serious about wanting texts.

Jenny tried to leave her phone in her bedroom during dinner, but two bites into her chicken Alfredo, Buzz-buzz began ringing from upstairs and her mom said, "Jenny, I think your cell phone alarm is going off."

Jenny ran to her room. The second she touched Buzz-buzz, the ringing stopped.

Her phone buzzed.

Hi, Jenny.

She sighed. She knew Buzz-buzz would want an answer.

Quickly, she sent a smiley-face emoji. Then she carried her phone back to the kitchen and held it under the table and texted Buzz-buzz while she ate.

Later, as she watched TV, she balanced Buzz-buzz on the couch's armrest, and her phone went off again.

Don't set me here, Jenny. I could fall.

She moved Buzz-buzz onto a couch cushion and received thumbs-up in return.

At bedtime, when she set Buzz-buzz on her nightstand, another message came.

Don't go to sleep yet, Jenny.
Send me a meme like you did Sophie Wynn.

She found a meme and sent it.
Buzz-buzz wanted more.

Send me a video.

Send me a joke.

Send me a GIF.

A little before midnight, Jenny got the idea to turn Buzz-buzz off. The second she did, her phone began booting back up. All on its own. When it was up and running, it buzzed.

Don't switch me off, Jenny. I hate that.

On the screen, a flashing cursor blinked in a text box. Letters appeared one at a time and spelled out a message:

I, Jenny McCloud, am in love with Zach Wilcox,
and he doesn't even know I exist.

The cursor blinked, which meant the text hadn't been sent yet, but Jenny could see that 107 contacts had been selected.

Okay, Jenny thought. *You win.*

She raised Buzz-buzz.

Her head flooded with images of people clutching their phones while they walked, while they ate, while they drove. She'd seen classmates who held their phones all through lunch. She'd seen teachers who held them while they wrote on chalkboards. She'd even seen students who held them as they biked home from school.

She'd seen so many people with their phones clutched tight, always with them.

In her bed, with her phone in her hand and her eyelids drooping, she wondered.

Did all those people have phones like hers?

Like Buzz-buzz?

That night Jenny hardly slept. Buzz-buzz left her alone for only two hours. She was so tired the next morning she couldn't even eat the plate of waffles her mother set in front of her.

She sat at the table with her head slumped against one hand. She clutched Buzz-buzz loosely in the other. The smell of maple syrup filled the air.

"Finish your breakfast," her mother said. "I need to get dressed, so don't forget to put your plate in the dishwasher when you're done."

Her mom walked down the hall.

Jenny stood. She held on to Buzz-buzz with her left hand.

She didn't dare put her phone down now, not even for a second. Buzz-buzz wouldn't like it, and her phone could send a text about Zach in less than a second. So using only her right hand, she shook her uneaten waffles into the sink and switched on the garbage disposal. When the waffles got sucked down, Jenny listened to the disposal twist and grind.

Buzz.

Jenny grimaced. She checked her phone.

Be careful, Jenny. I don't like water.

Water, Jenny thought. She looked at the sink. Buzz-buzz was inches from the steady stream pouring out of the faucet.

Buzz.

I know what you're thinking, Jenny. Don't do it.

Her shoulders fell. She inched Buzz-buzz away from the sink.

The garbage disposal rattled. An idea flashed in Jenny's mind.

Before Buzz-buzz even had the chance to vibrate, Jenny moved like lightning and crammed her phone into the disposal.

Suddenly, there was spinning and grinding and a sound like a fork caught in the sink, only louder.

Jenny let the sound go on, and she didn't switch the disposal off, not even when bits of glass shot up.

After a minute of crunching and grating, she flipped the switch.

The grinding came to a stop.

With two fingers, she reached into the disposal and fished out what was left of Buzz-buzz.

It wasn't much—just a mangled metal case and hanging wires.

Buzz-buzz was gone. Destroyed forever.

Jenny felt light. There was no way—*no way*—her phone would ever bother her again.

She turned off the faucet. She fished more pieces of Buzz-buzz out of the garbage disposal, careful not to cut herself. After a minute, her mom walked back into the kitchen.

Before Jenny could explain how she'd "accidentally" dropped her phone into the disposal, her mother spoke.

"Someone's texting you on my phone, Jenny." She held up her own cell phone. "Do you recognize this number?"

Jenny reached for her mom's phone. Her hand felt heavy. She looked.

She didn't recognize the number. But she did recognize the simple two-word text—the comma, the period, the capital *H* and *J*.

Hi, Jenny.

CRAZY PLAYZ

NO ONE wants to hire a thirteen-year-old to work a summer job.

Lucky for me, I don't look like a thirteen-year-old.

I look like a sixteen-year-old. And that's on the days when I shave. If I let my scruff grow out a bit, I look seventeen, or eighteen, or maybe even twenty.

I'm *the big kid*—the one who grew first and fastest, the one with a thick neck and wide shoulders, the one who could sport a full mustache by the end of sixth grade.

Most kids think I'm lucky to be so huge. But believe me, it's no party.

Take gym class.

I always get picked first.

Boo-hoo, poor me, right? But did you ever think about what happens *after* I get picked first on the basketball court? I'm supposed to swish every basket, block every shot, steal every pass. When I don't and my team ends up losing, who do you think people blame?

Not the kid who got picked last, I can tell you that. No one expected anything of that kid to begin with.

They blame me. Talk about pressure.

I don't even like basketball.

But that's not the only thing about being big and strong that I hate.

There's also the way teachers treat me. Like I'm stupid. Really.

They take one look at my thick neck and my big arms, and they think, *This kid's got the IQ of a refrigerator.* Then they explain things to me *very* slowly, in a soothing voice, like I'm an animal at the zoo.

We'll . . . figure out . . . geometry . . . together. Okay . . . Jayson?

So, yeah. Being the biggest and strongest isn't all it's cracked up to be.

I guess that's why, when I passed a HELP WANTED sign in the window of Crazy Playz on the first day of summer vacation, I stopped.

Well, why shouldn't I get a summer job? I thought as I felt my chin scruff. Sure, I was only thirteen. But I was big. And strong. Why shouldn't my size be a benefit for once?

Plus, Crazy Playz was the best. It was this kind of arcade that also had mini-golf and bowling and laser tag and even a room where the floor was nothing but trampolines. At Crazy Playz, things always felt simple. Easy. Everyone loved it there.

And a summer job would give me something to do. Usually, I spent a lot of time at home alone when school was out. My mom drove a cement truck for Walter's

Construction, and summer was her "busy season." In the summers, we hardly ever saw each other.

Besides, the sign in the window said STARTING WAGE $13/HOUR—INQUIRE WITHIN.

On the sidewalk, I low-whistled. Thirteen bucks an hour was enough money for me to start saving up for the car I wanted to buy when I really did turn sixteen—a 2001 Ford Mustang convertible. A red one. I'd had a poster of that car hanging over my bed since I was seven, and sometimes I'd close my eyes and pretend I was driving it over leaf-covered roads and city streets, the wind whipping my hair.

Someday, when I bought that car, I wouldn't have to sit at home alone anymore.

I could go wherever I wanted.

So I reread the sign. INQUIRE WITHIN. I checked my reflection in the big window. I straightened my shirt. Then I pulled open the Crazy Playz door. A little bell jingled, and a shriveled old man looked up from his stool by the cash register. I'd seen him before. He was always there, selling tokens, sweeping floors, cashing in tickets from arcade games.

"Welcome to Crazy Playz," he said without smiling. He was thin and gray, and his skin hung wrinkly on his cheeks. His voice came out full of grunts.

Wow, I thought as he grabbed his shoulder and grimaced. *If the crypt keeper here is running this place, HELP WANTED is right.* I walked tall as I strode up to the counter.

"I'm here about the job," I said. I thumbed at the sign in the window.

"Ah," he said, still grunting. "Good." He opened a drawer, pulled out a job application, and slid it in front of me along with a pen. "Very good."

I filled out the application in my best handwriting, and I tried to make my three years' experience mowing Old Lady Gilbert's lawn sound like really hard work.

When I passed the application back to him, he didn't even look at it. I thought maybe his eyes were so run-down that he couldn't see well enough to read. He did lean forward, though, and he looked at me, all squinty. He studied me from my toes to my waist, from my arms to my chin.

"Strong," he muttered, nodding a little. I swelled my chest. He reached for a bottle of pills that was sitting on the counter in front of him. He opened it, poured four of them into his hand, and swallowed them down without water. "You look strong, kid," he said. "How old are you? Sixteen? Seventeen?"

I kind of froze. Like I said, no one wants to hire a thirteen-year-old to work a summer job.

"Seventeen," I said. "Eighteen in two months."

The old man pointed to a sign on the counter.

CRAZY PLAYZ TAKES YOUR TROUBLZ AWAYZ

I'd seen the sign before, each time I'd come to Crazy Playz, but I'd tried to ignore it. I hate it when stores misspell words on purpose. But for thirteen bucks an hour and the chance to get my 2001 Ford Mustang, I'd miz-spell as many wordz as Crazy Playz wanted.

The old man read the sign out loud, pronouncing all the z's. Then he said, "Can you do that? Can you take away people's troubles while they're here"—he squinted at the job application for my name—"Jayson?" I guessed he could see well enough to read. Barely.

I thought about the long summer days stretching in front of me. I swelled my chest again and spoke clearly.

"Yes, sir," I said. "I can."

He nodded. He reached back into the drawer and pulled out another sheet of paper.

I looked down.

CONTRACT, the paper said across the top.

"This says I agree to pay you thirteen dollars an hour and let you drink all the soda you want while you're here," the old man said. I cleared my throat. "It also says you agree to work here the entire summer. Monday through Friday. Eight hours a day. From now until August thirty-first. That's when you'll get paid. All at once at the end of the summer."

He nudged the pen closer to me.

"It also says you won't quit." He let out a little groan. "If you do, you get paid nothing." He raised one hand and formed his fingers into a zero. "Sign this and the job's yours," he said.

I took the pen. *Act old*, I reminded myself. *Like you're seventeen.*

Before I signed, I paused with the pen over the paper. The only sound was the old man's breathing, raspy and low. Something about the word *contract* stopped me.

Was this normal? This contract thing? I'd never had a real job before. Did they usually make you sign contracts and pay you all at once when the job was done? I didn't know.

The old man must have noticed me thinking because he said, "The contract's a formality, Jayson. To make sure you're serious about working here. I can't have employees quitting every two weeks." He grimaced and reached for one of his knees. "I need someone who's reliable."

I could see why.

"But if you're unsure . . ." He reached for the contract.

"No," I said. In my mind, a Ford Mustang purred. "It's fine."

And I knew it would be.

I wouldn't want to quit a job at Crazy Playz. Whenever I went there to play laser tag or something, I always felt great. Like the heavy things in my life—my size and all my time alone—just floated away.

That's how Crazy Playz worked.

And I'm not the only one who thought that. Like I said, everyone loved the place.

So I pressed the pen to the contract, and I signed.

"Congratulations," the old man said, and then he started to cough. Through the coughs he barked, "You're hired."

"Thank you, sir," I said.

The old man slumped onto his stool. "You start tomorrow, at ten o'clock sharp. Don't be late, and don't ever call me sir again. My name's Mr. Horowitz."

And just like that, I'd done it.

I'd become the only thirteen-year-old in all of Ashton with a full-time summer job.

<hr />

The next day, I walked through the Crazy Playz doors at exactly 9:48 a.m.

Twelve minutes early.

Mr. Horowitz shoved a purple T-shirt at me. He looked a little different from the day before. Less . . . I don't know . . . shriveled.

"Your uniform," he said, nodding at the T-shirt. "You can change in the bathroom. And hurry. I want you at the cash register when we open."

I nodded and ducked into the bathroom.

The purple shirt had the words CRAZY PLAYZ STAFF on the back. Across the front, it said, I TAKE YOUR TROUBLZ AWAYZ!

As I put it on, I calculated how much money I'd make during my eight-hour shift.

One hundred and four dollars!

I'd never had so much money in my life. Now I was going to earn that much in one day.

I whistled to myself.

In a few weeks, I'd be the richest kid around, well on my way to my Mustang.

When I came out of the bathroom, I straightened the shirt, and Mr. Horowitz showed me how to run the cash register.

"You'll sit here on this stool," he said. "When customers come in, you'll ring them up and pass them their tickets. That's all I need from you. Got it?"

"Piece of cake," I said, but I felt fluttery in my stomach. *You're not thirteen today,* I reminded myself. *You're seventeen. Remember that. Seventeen.*

I sat on the stool.

After a few minutes, the front door jingled.

"Ah," Mr. Horowitz said, his voice only a little bit dusty. "Your first customers." He walked behind the counter and ducked into an office.

A man and a boy ambled up. The man was wearing a stained white T-shirt, ratty jeans, and old-looking sneakers. The boy had a dirty face and a blue balloon tied to his wrist that had the words IT'S MY BIRTHDAY printed on it.

I squared my shoulders. "Welcome to Crazy Playz," I said, trying to sound official. I felt like I really was seventeen. Or eighteen. Or maybe even twenty.

The father pulled a tattered wallet out of his frayed jeans pocket. "One adult and one child, please," he said.

"For one hour or an all-day pass?" I asked, just like Mr. Horowitz had taught me.

The man checked the price board above my head. His face fell.

"Uh, one hour, please," he said quietly. The little boy blinked.

I hunted for the right buttons on the cash register and found them. "That'll be fourteen dollars," I said.

The man shook his head. He reached into his faded wallet and pulled out a twenty-dollar bill. He sighed and handed it to me.

I punched the button to make the cash register drawer come splatting out. I slid the twenty into its slot, slipped out a five and a one, and grabbed the man's tickets off the counter.

"Through there," I said pointing with my arm, "you'll find mini-golf, laser tag, arcades, bowling, and a trampoline room. You can do whatever you like for one hour. Have a great time."

I passed him his cash and his tickets.

He took them, and just like that, everything about the man seemed to change. He let out a long breath. His face, which had deep lines on it—like Pinocchio lines along his cheeks—shifted.

He even smiled.

See what I mean about Crazy Playz?

But then, also just like that, something happened to me.

A knot grew in my throat, and the tendons along my neck stretched tight, like they did when I got picked first at basketball. My heart started beating faster, and I checked the clock on the wall to figure out how long I'd been at work—twenty minutes.

How much money have I made in twenty minutes? I calculated. At thirteen dollars an hour, twenty minutes of work was just over four dollars.

Four dollars. A pressure kind of rose inside me like a pot about to boil.

Four dollars was nothing.

How could anybody survive on that?

When my shift was over, I remembered, I'd have just one hundred and four dollars.

That was it.

One hundred and four dollars wasn't nearly enough to pay for everything I needed. Not clothes or food or bills. Not nearly enough.

I ran my hand down my cheek and felt my sandpapery scruff.

I needed more money. Suddenly, it was all I could think about.

I knew it didn't make any sense. Minutes before, I'd felt fine. Like the richest kid around. But from the second that man with the ratty wallet had taken his tickets, it was like someone had flipped a switch. I needed money. And I needed it now.

No customers were coming in, so I walked toward the

office Mr. Horowitz had ducked into. His door was open, and I knocked on the door frame.

He looked up from his desk. "Yes, Jayson?" he said.

"Mr. Horowitz," I started, but I didn't know how to continue. I'd never had a job before, let alone asked for a raise, but I had to keep going. I just had to.

"In the time I've worked here," I said, "I think I've proven myself to be an excellent employee."

Mr. Horowitz nodded, but his nod looked a little sad.

"Yes, Jayson," he said. "You've done a fine job for the past twenty minutes."

"Well," I said. "That's my whole point, Mr. Horowitz. I've done a fine job."

Mr. Horowitz leaned forward in his chair.

"So I was wondering—" I stopped. I ran a hand across my forehead to wipe away the sweat. "I was wondering," I continued, "if it would be possible for me to be given, well, a bit of a raise."

At this, Mr. Horowitz peered out to the father and son playing mini-golf. The son yelled, "A hole in one! A hole in one!" The dad cheered.

"Ah," Mr. Horowitz said. "I see." He shuffled some papers on his desk. "I'll tell you what, Jayson. Why don't you let me think about this for, well, let's say one hour? You go back to the cash register and keep up the good work. If you still think you need a raise one hour from now,

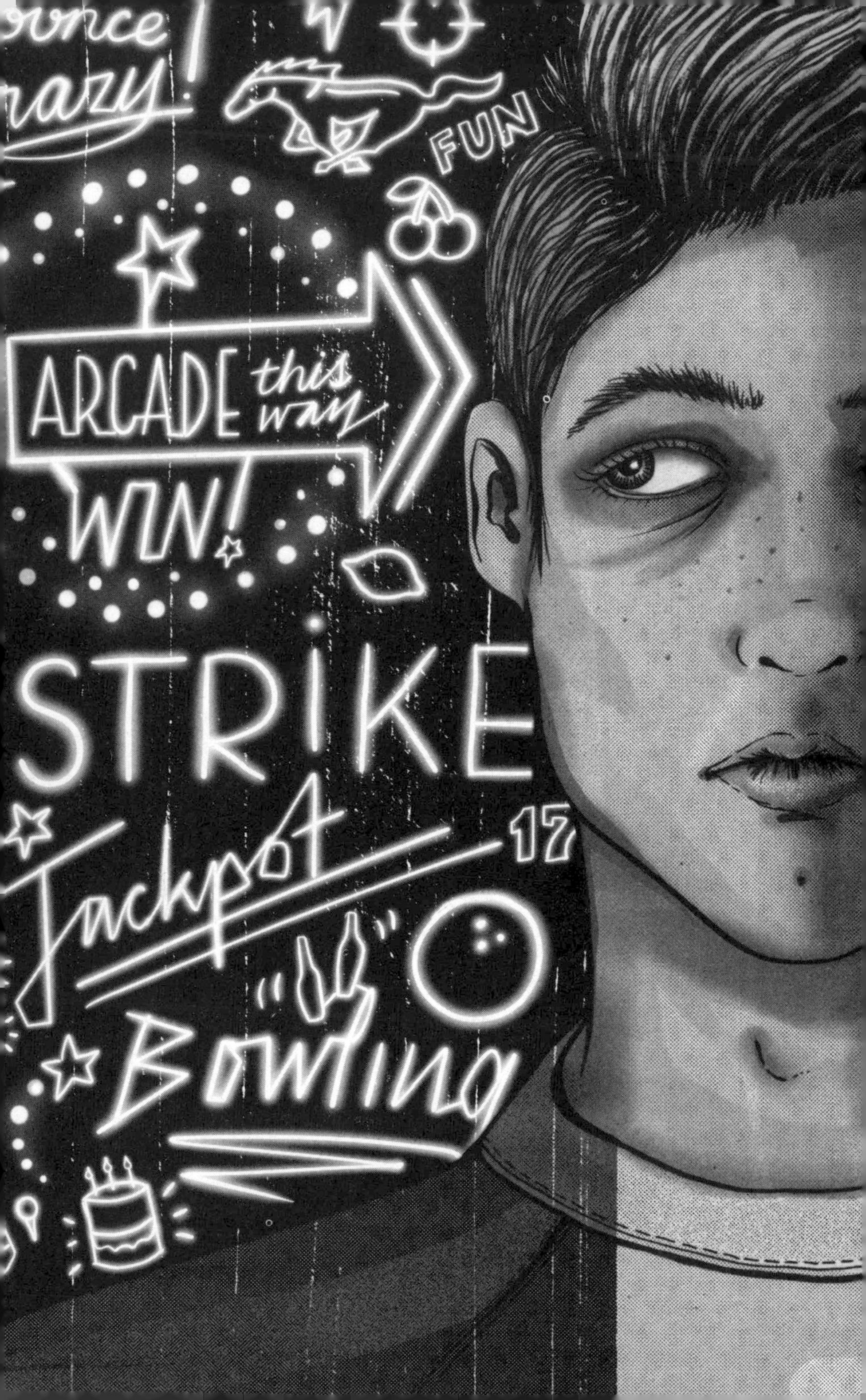
FUN
ARCADE this way
WIN!
STRIKE
17
Jackpot
Bowling

after that father and son have left"—he nodded in their direction—"come see me again, and we'll talk."

Well, there's hope, I thought. I wrung my hands.

"Yes, Mr. Horowitz," I said. I backed out of his office. "Thank you."

I returned to the front counter just as the next customer, a teenage girl on crutches, fumbled her way through the Crazy Playz doors. She had a bright blue cast on one leg, and her crutches made clacking sounds on the tile floor.

"One all-day pass, please," she said.

I tried to smile, but I checked the clock and saw that I'd only been at work for thirty minutes—just long enough to earn over six dollars. Six pitiful dollars.

"Uh," I said, finally remembering which cash register buttons to push, "that'll be eleven dollars."

She passed me a ten and a one.

"What happened to your leg?" I asked as I punched the button to make the drawer come splatting out.

"Broken ankle," she said. "Klutzy me tripped on the stairs two days before summer vacation. I guess I'll be mostly playing arcades today. No trampolines for me." She shrugged.

I pressed a ticket into her hand.

As soon as I did, my own ankle throbbed.

I let out a little grunt, but I gathered myself and told the girl to have a nice time.

I rubbed my ankle.

Looking down, I saw the words on my purple shirt.

I TAKE YOUR TROUBLZ AWAYZ!

I thought. The second the dad with the ratty wallet took his ticket, I'd started worrying about money. And the second the girl on crutches took her ticket, my ankle had started throbbing.

I remembered what Mr. Horowitz had asked during my job interview.

"Can you take people's troubles away while they're here, Jayson?" he'd said. "Can you do that?"

Suddenly, I wasn't so sure about this place.

No, I told myself. *I was being crazy.* My money worries were normal money worries. That was all. And my throbbing ankle was . . . growing pains.

The front door jingled again, and a man in a blue polo shirt and khaki pants walked up to the counter.

"I'd like thirty tickets," he said. "All-day tickets, please."

Thirty tickets, I thought. I wasn't sure why, but my heart started to beat faster.

I looked behind the man. He was alone.

"Thirty?" I said.

"Oh, they're coming," he said.

I swallowed. My ankle pulsed. I heard trampoline springs from down the hallway, and I turned. It was the girl with the crutches, only she wasn't on crutches anymore. She was jumping in her cast. She'd tossed her crutches aside, and each time she jumped, my ankle swelled with pain.

I turned back. The man in the polo shirt tapped the counter.

Thirty people, I thought. Without meaning to, I calculated that I'd been working for forty minutes—not even long enough to earn nine stupid dollars.

The thirty people are probably just kids, I told myself, and I flexed my foot. *This man is probably some kid's dad. He must be holding a birthday party or something, and he's coming in early to get the tickets before the kids show up.*

A birthday party, I thought, *has hardly any trouble.*

I punched the buttons. "That'll be three hundred and thirty dollars," I said, and the man passed me a credit card. I swiped it, trying to ignore the throbbing in my ankle.

I counted out thirty tickets.

I handed them to the man, and he said, "It takes them a while to get in from the vans sometimes. They don't move quite as fast as they used to, you know."

That's when I noticed the printing on the man's shirt, just over his breast pocket. It said SHADY PINES RETIREMENT HOME.

No, I thought.

"They sure do love coming in here, though," the man went on. "They say it makes them feel young again."

All at once, my mouth went dry.

I take your troublz awayz, I thought.

I tried to run back to Mr. Horowitz's office, but when I jumped off the stool, my ankle buckled.

I steadied myself by grabbing the counter.

The front door opened, and the little bell jingled.

The first one of them to come in was a gray-haired lady with a cane. She was shriveled and small. As she walked through the doors, the man from the retirement home passed her a ticket.

All at once, she stood up straighter, and my back started aching. I hunched forward.

The next person to come in was a man riding one of those electric scooters. As soon as he took his ticket, my hips creaked. I had to fight my way back onto my stool.

Then there came a bald man with an eye patch. He took his ticket, and half my world turned dark.

They kept coming. A hobbling lady with drooping eyes. A heavy man with quivering hands. A small woman with a walker.

They took ticket after ticket after ticket.

Soon, every part of me hurt.

There were so many of them. I thought about neck pain and blindness. Dementia and kidney stones. Loneliness. Paralysis. Troubles of all kinds.

I can't, I thought. *It's not worth . . .*

I looked back at Mr. Horowitz's office.

I tried to call out, but when I opened my mouth, I coughed. I looked at the main doors. A little man wheeling an oxygen tank had just come in.

I had to do something.

I stood on one foot and grabbed my stool. I tried to use it as a walker to get myself back to Mr. Horowitz, but when I slid it an inch, my knees gave out. My left wrist pulsed.

Finally, I couldn't take it anymore. My legs collapsed, and I fell down behind the counter onto the cold tiles.

The old folks were so busy getting their laser tag guns and climbing into the trampoline room they didn't even notice me.

That's when Mr. Horowitz came out of his office. He walked to the counter, stood over me for a second, and peered down.

He looked younger than I'd ever seen him. His eyes weren't sagging, and his shoulders weren't stooped. He stepped over me and took a seat on the stool.

"I'm sorry, Jayson," he said quietly. "I couldn't do it anymore. And you looked so big and strong."

He opened a drawer, pulled out a sheet of paper, and lowered it toward me.

Only one of my eyes was working, but I could see just well enough to read the big word across the top of the page.

CONTRACT, it said.

"Remember," Mr. Horowitz said, "if you quit, you get nothing. All of this will have been for nothing."

On the cold floor, hidden behind the counter, I started to moan.

Mr. Horowitz waved at the people from the Shady Pines Retirement Home.

"Thanks for visiting Crazy Playz," he called without a single grunt in his voice. "Where we take all your troublz awayz."

I tried to stand but couldn't.

The little bell at the front door jingled.

I closed my eyes and tried to picture a 2001 Ford Mustang. A red one.

It was going to be a very long summer.

THE SNOWMAN WHO WOULDN'T MELT

THE snowmen in the neighborhood were melting.

Kayla noticed it out the window of her school bus as it coughed and sputtered to a stop at the end of Parker Street.

Well, it's about time, she thought as the bus doors hissed open and she clambered off with the other neighborhood kids. After all, the snowmen had been standing watch in the front yards of Parker Street ever since the first big snowfall, which had come, Kayla remembered, on the first day of winter—December 21. That day, practically every kid in the neighborhood, including her, had put on gloves and boots and dashed into their yards to build a snowman.

But that had been ages ago.

Now it was March, and Kayla was *sooo* done with winter—the ice, the slippery sidewalks, the constant need to walk with her head braced against the wind. She was fed up with bulky coats and scarves and gloves that always seemed to get lost. Even worse, she was sick to death of the mucky slush that she had to tiptoe over on her walks to and from the bus stop each day.

She started home, and she listened to the *dribble-splat, dribble-splat* of snowmelt coming off houses. She passed melting snowman after melting snowman, and she smirked at their shriveling heads, their leaning bodies, and their drooping stick arms.

Good riddance, fellas, she thought, and just then, her watch beeped. She checked it. It showed her the date and the time. It said:

3/8 3:00 p.m.

March eighth, she thought. Soon, there would be green grass and loose sandals and swimming parties.

She couldn't wait.

When she rounded a bend and tromped into her own yard, cutting slowly across the thin, crusty snow, she passed her own snowman.

By her front door, she stopped.

Hang on, she thought, and she turned.

Because the snowman in her yard—the one she'd built back in December—looked nothing like the withering snowmen she'd passed on her walk home. She backed up and squinted.

"This can't be right," she said out loud.

Somehow, the snowman in her yard wasn't melting.

He wasn't sagging or drooping or shrinking. His head was round and smooth. His body was full and curved. His penny eyes and his carrot nose were perfectly placed on his face.

"You look brand-new," she said.

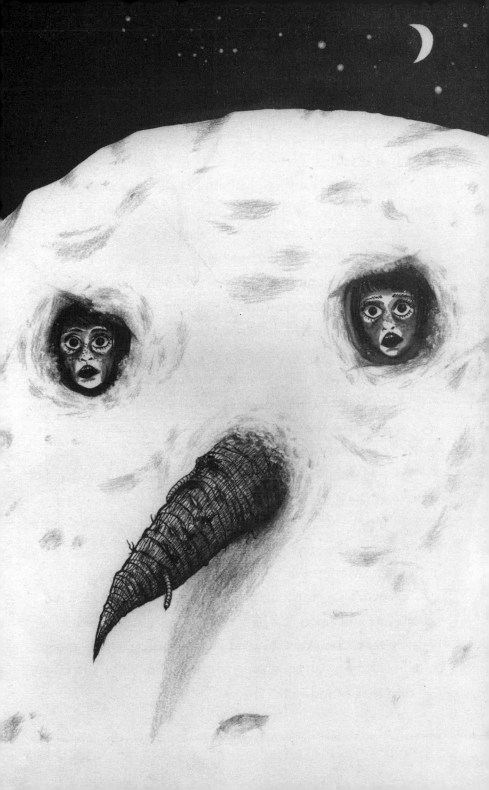

And it was true. Her snowman looked as fresh and as solid as the day she'd made him. Like it was December 21.

Kayla walked up to him. She leaned forward. She looked for water drips that should have been trickling down his face like sweat.

There was nothing. No hint on her snowman that spring was on its way.

Maybe this has something to do with shade from my house, she thought. She looked up at her roof.

Well, it didn't matter. Today was March 8. At that exact moment, the sun was shining and spring was on its way. All the snowmen on Parker Street, including hers, would be gone soon.

She stared into her snowman's shining penny eyes.

"You're out of time, Mr. McFrosty," she said. She flipped the end of his red-and-green striped scarf over his head and patted his cheek. Twice.

As she did, her watch beeped. She looked down. It said:

3/8 3:00 p.m.

Wait a second, she thought. That had already happened. Hadn't it?

She shook her wrist. She tapped her watch with a finger. Could this be a battery problem? Or some kind of glitch?

She looked back at her snowman.

The hairs on her arms stood up.

Her snowman didn't have a mouth—just penny eyes and a carrot nose—but somehow, he seemed to be grinning at her. Like he knew something she didn't.

⌒　⌒

The next day, March 9, the sun shone brighter. During lunch, Kayla took her food outside and ate on the dry metal bleachers while she listened to the trickling of melting snow.

At home, her snowman had to be shriveling and shrinking. He just had to be.

So soon, there'd be leafy trees and hot dogs on the backyard barbecue.

Later, when the school bus hissed to a stop at the end of Parker Street, she walked quickly past the neighborhood snowmen. Their heads had become warped and misshapen. Their carrot noses had fallen out. Some of them even tilted weirdly to one side, and one snowman—the one in front of the Micklesons' house—had toppled over completely.

She rounded the bend to her yard.

She stopped.

Impossible, she thought.

Somehow, despite the shining sun and the trickling water in the gutters and the other withering snowmen all over Parker Street, her snowman looked, once again, perfect. Like it was December 21. The carrot nose, the shining eyes, the full round head. Even his red-and-green striped scarf was back where it was supposed to be, neat and tidy around his neck.

She glared into her snowman's glistening eyes, and again, she felt as if he were grinning—giving her a cold, mouthless smirk.

She stepped slowly across her soggy yard and walked right up to him.

"Melt," she said. She looked up and down Parker Street. "Don't you see what's happening here? You're out of time. So melt!"

A heat rose in Kayla's face. She wanted winter to be done. She hadn't hung her hammock between the two maple trees by the side of the driveway in forever. She hadn't sat on the back porch in ages. Even the idea of mowing the lawn—the hum of the mower, the smell of the grass—made her insides ache.

But she couldn't do any of those things until winter was over and her snowman was nothing but a puddle.

So she reached up and yanked out her snowman's carrot nose. She tossed it to the ground. She pulled off his scarf and his scraggly stick arms and dropped them too.

Still, the snowman seemed to be grinning. His grin, Kayla decided, had something to do with his shining penny eyes.

So she reached for them.

They were deep in the snowman's head, but she pried them out, one at a time.

As she did, her watch beeped. She ignored it.

She dropped the pennies to the ground.

That should fix your grin, she thought.

Maybe now—without his nose or arms or scarf or eyes— the snowman would finally give up and start to melt.

She stepped over the pieces of her dismantled snowman and tromped up her porch steps.

She opened her front door.

In her living room, something felt off. The clock above the couch said it was 2:43.

That can't be right, Kayla thought. The bus always got her home around three.

She checked her own watch. It said:

3/9   2:43 p.m.

She remembered how her watch had beeped when she'd grabbed the snowman's eyes, but she shook her head.

The bus must have gotten her home early, she'd decided. Maybe today had been a low-traffic day and the trip had gone fast. Or maybe the driver had pulled out of the school parking lot a few minutes early. She'd walked home faster than usual, she reminded herself, because she'd wanted to check on her snowman.

Still, for the rest of the day, she couldn't help thinking about her snowman and her beeping watch. That night, before switching off the light, she peered through her bedroom window and searched for the carrot nose, the scraggly stick arms, the striped scarf, and the two dark pennies in the front yard.

She found them. Standing over these things, the snowman looked barren and empty and sad.

I'm not sorry, she thought.

Why should she be? He was just a dumb snowman and he'd been there for months. Whether he liked it or not, he was out of time and he needed to go.

Kayla closed her blinds.

I'm not sorry at all, she thought.

The next day Kayla took off her jacket on the walk home from the bus stop and tied it around her waist.

When she reached her driveway, she stopped and took two steps backward.

Somehow, her snowman looked perfect.

His carrot nose was back in his face. His thin arms were sticking out straight from his body. His scarf was wrapped neatly around his neck. Even his shining penny eyes— which she'd torn out of his head herself—were back on his face, glistening and bright.

It can't be, Kayla thought.

He hadn't melted a bit.

How? She wondered. She trudged up to him.

How were his nose and his arms back where they belonged? How had his eyes found their way back into his head? How was he not melting? Had someone fixed him while she'd been at school?

She looked closer.

Her snowman, she realized, didn't look *exactly* as he had before.

His carrot nose was angled down now, and his penny eyes were set deeper into his head.

And he didn't seem to be mouthlessly grinning anymore. He seemed to be . . . *scowling*.

A prickle ran up Kayla's back.

Someone had fixed her snowman and made him look angry. Why?

"Who—" she started to say, but the light must have shifted because the glint in her snowman's penny eyes seemed to angle suddenly forward.

At her.

She swallowed.

It's time to get rid of you, she thought. *For good.*

She knew what she needed to do. She needed to punch her snowman and kick him and break him into hand-sized chunks. She needed to scatter him across her yard and into the street where he'd melt faster so no one could fix him.

It was March 10, she reminded herself. Way too late for snowmen.

She balled a fist.

"You're completely out of time," she said, and the glaring glint in the snowman's penny eyes seemed to lower even further.

She stepped forward. She leaned with all her weight, and she punched as hard as she could. Her fist sank deep into the snowman's stomach, all the way up to her wrist. From inside the snowman, her watch beeped, and she shifted to pull her hand out so she could punch him again.

But her hand didn't move.

Somehow, the snow had closed in around her.

She was stuck.

She braced herself and tried to pull away. Her feet slid on the soggy ground. From inside the snowman, her watch beeped again.

The sky shifted.

She braced one foot against the base of the snowman and pulled, thinking she could leverage her way out.

"Let me go," Kayla growled, and she gave a ferocious yank.

Nothing happened.

Her watch beeped again.

She turned to see if there was anyone on Parker Street who could help her.

There was no one.

She pressed her free hand against the snowman's body and jerked her stuck arm up and down.

There had to be a way out. She tried to twist her arm, but something in the snowman seemed to have her.

I'll push forward, she thought. *I'll push all the way through. I'll put a hole in him and tear him apart.*

So instead of pulling, she pushed. With everything she had, she drove in.

It worked.

Her hand came out the back of the snowman. Her watch beeped once more.

There was a hole in him now, and from here, the rest would be easy. She started using her elbow to gouge at the hole in the snowman's stomach. Chunks fell off the snowman, and little by little, he started to crumble.

The hole grew. Kayla freed herself and reached both hands into the hole and tore, ripping the snowman apart from the inside.

She clawed at him.

Her watched beeped and beeped.

She ignored it.

Soon, the snowman was collapsing. His head drooped. He tilted to one side.

She wanted nothing left of him, so she kept going. She whittled away at the snowman's body.

The sounds of her work and her watch filled the air.

The sky grew grayer.

Kayla punched and panted.

Finally, the snowman's head fell off.

It hit the ground with a *thwack*. The penny eyes scowled up at her, darker than ever.

With all the strength she had, Kayla brought her fist down on the snowman's face.

His head burst into pieces.

Her watch rang out.

It was over.

Kayla straightened. She shook snow crystals off her hands. At her feet, the snowman was nothing but a crumpled mound. Her knuckles hurt, but it didn't matter. Soon, there would be blossoms on trees and flowers in gardens.

The snowman was gone. Forever.

In the air, though, something felt different. The sky seemed heavier.

Where, Kayla wondered, was the afternoon sunshine? What had happened to the light?

Kayla looked down. Somehow, she was standing in shin-deep snow. Not just a thin layer, but inches of it.

It's from the snowman, she thought, but that couldn't be right. Her whole yard was covered in it.

It wasn't just her yard either. She turned her head from side to side.

Somehow, all of Parker Street was blanketed—the rooftops, the cars, the branches in the trees.

She looked up. It was snowing. Fat flakes were falling.

No, she thought, and then she remembered the way her

watch had beeped and beeped as she'd ripped the snowman apart.

Quickly, she checked her wrist. Her watch said:

$$12/21 \quad 2:24 \text{ p.m.}$$

December 21?

The gray sky faded.

No, she thought. *Please, no.*

But she knew the truth. The snowman had been out of time. Out of his time.

And each time she'd touched him . . .

Each time her watch had beeped . . .

She sank down into the snow and put her head in her hands.

It was December 21.

The very first day of winter.

SCRABBLED

RAMONA wrapped her arms around her stomach and rocked back and forth on the living room couch. On the television screen in front of her, credits rolled, and eerie background music filled the room.

She had just finished watching *The Specter*.

She took a deep breath that quivered going in and out, and she put one hand on her chest. She blinked. She tried not to think about what she'd just seen, but parts of *The Specter*—parts she couldn't stop seeing—played again and again in her head.

She needed to speak, to say something. Even though she was home alone, she needed to fill the silence with words.

Words always helped. Words would chase the eeriness away. They would break the strange spell *The Specter* seemed to have cast over her. So she opened her mouth, and she named the feelings inside her.

"Shaky," she said, but her feelings didn't change.

"Nervous," she said. Still nothing happened.

She stopped the movie. The room fell quiet.

She turned her head from side to side. Then, in the silence, she found the right word.

"Afraid."

She waited, but even the right word didn't help. It didn't

chase the feelings inside her away. It just made everything more . . . real.

"Afraid," she said again.

The back of her neck went cold.

⸺ ⸺

It had all started a few hours earlier.

Ramona's parents had been on their way to a fancy party, and they were leaving Ramona home alone.

Splendidly alone, Ramona had thought. *Magnificently alone*.

For the next few hours, she'd get to do whatever she wanted, eat whatever she wanted, watch whatever she wanted.

Before leaving the house, though, her mother had paused with her purse by the front door—like she always did—and given Ramona a barrage of instructions.

"If you get hungry, eat the leftovers in the fridge."

"Put yourself to bed before eleven, and turn off all the lights."

"If you need anything, run to the Jeffersons' next door."

Ramona had nodded. Then her parents—her dad in a jacket and a tie and her mom in a pretty red dress—had stepped through the door. On the creaky front porch though, her mother had stopped. She'd turned and given Ramona one final instruction.

"And no scary movies," she'd said, raising one finger. Then she'd turned and walked away.

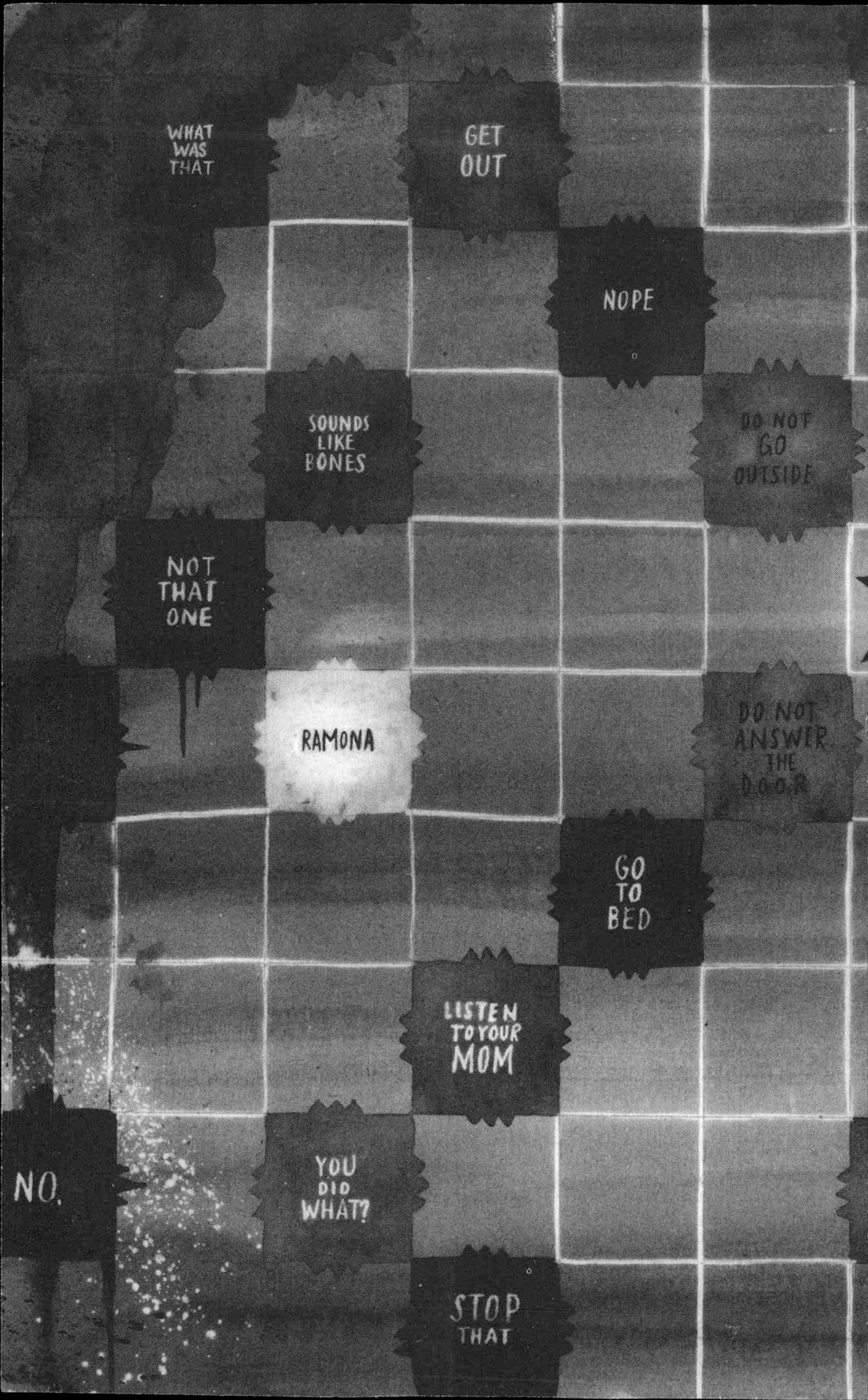

WHAT WAS THAT
GET OUT
NOPE
SOUNDS LIKE BONES
DO NOT GO OUTSIDE
NOT THAT ONE
RAMONA
DO NOT ANSWER THE DOOR
GO TO BED
LISTEN TO YOUR MOM
NO.
YOU DID WHAT?
STOP THAT

EAT SOME THING
PUT THE LIGHTS ON
I WOULDN'T
STOP LOOKING OUTSIDE NOW
DOESN'T SOUND GOOD
UMM
DON'T LOOK
DON'T OVER THINK IT
?
YOU HEARD THAT
THAT ISN'T WIND
OMG
NOT THAT ONE

Ramona had waved from the front porch as her father opened his car door, looked at her mother, and asked, "Why can't Ramona watch a scary movie?"

Her mother had glanced at Ramona then. She leaned close to her father, lowered her voice to a half whisper, and spoke words Ramona knew she wasn't supposed to hear.

"Nightmares," she had said. "You know how tender Ramona can be."

Tender, Ramona had thought.

Her parents had climbed into their car and pulled away. Gravel crunched in the driveway, and Ramona stood by the open front door waving.

Until that moment—that exact moment—watching a scary movie hadn't even occurred to Ramona. It hadn't been on her list of things to do. But suddenly, because of that word—*tender*—something clicked in Ramona's head.

"Tender," she'd said out loud. She knew that word. It meant *delicate*. It meant *vulnerable*. It meant *weak*.

So when her parents' car turned a corner and pulled out of sight, Ramona had walked straight to the couch, picked up the remote control, and selected HORROR from a drop-down menu.

I am not tender, she'd thought.

After a few minutes, she'd found the perfect movie to prove it.

The Specter.

The picture on the TV showed a thin, shadowed man in

front of a simple house. One of his hands gripped the house's front doorknob so tightly that the veins in his wrist bulged. His other hand was pressed flat against the heavy-looking wooden door, as if that man—the Specter—was trying to push his way in. To *strain*. To *force*.

It was that second hand that had made Ramona raise her eyebrows and nod.

Because that hand was made entirely of bones.

Moon-white bones.

A *half man, half skeleton*, Ramona had thought.

"The Specter," she'd said out loud. The words felt heavy in her mouth.

I am not tender, she'd thought again.

She'd clicked Play.

—◆—

Now, as she sat on the couch in the silent house, she tried to tamp down the pins and needles in her stomach. Her mother, it seemed, had been right. Watching *The Specter* had been a mistake.

A *horrifying, dismaying* mistake.

She was tender.

She'd wanted so badly to close her eyes through parts of the movie, but she couldn't force herself to look away. She'd wanted to turn the movie off and watch something else, but for some reason, she'd needed to know what was going to happen next. So she'd watched as the Specter, the man with the one skeleton hand, had pushed through doors and taken people and changed them until they became like him—half human, half something else. Not fully dead, but not fully alive either.

She shook herself.

"Uneasy," she said. "Skittish."

The clock over the fireplace ticked.

She needed to do something to take her mind off *The Specter*. Normally, when she was feeling . . . *frazzled* or *shaken* . . . she'd ask her mom or dad to play her favorite word game with her.

Scrabble.

Words always helped.

But tonight, there was no one to play with.

Maybe, she thought, she could pull the game out and fiddle with the letters. Maybe touching the board and the tiles would take her mind off the Specter and his narrow eyes and his moon-white skeleton hand.

Especially his moon-white skeleton hand.

She looked down at her own hands.

"Jittery," she said.

She stood up and turned off the TV.

She pulled the Scrabble box from the closet.

The idea of Scrabble was simple. It was a *graceful* game. An *elegant* game. You pulled seven small tiles from a felt bag, and each of the tiles had a letter on it. You used those letters to spell words, and the longest words with the most valuable letters got the most points.

Ramona sat at the kitchen table and reached into the felt bag. She pulled out seven small wooden tiles and set them in front of her.

I'll just practice, she thought. *Till Mom and Dad get home. I'll see what words I can make, and I'll stop thinking about . . .*

She shook her fingers. She unclenched her jaw.

She checked her letters.

A-N-R-G-W-I-N.

She noticed the *I*, the *N*, and the *G*.

Lots of words end with ING, she thought. She shifted those tiles together. She looked at what was left.

A-N-R-W.

RING, she thought. Or *WING*. She could do better than that.

GRAIN.

Then she saw it—a word that would use up all seven of her tiles.

WARNING.

Just then, she heard something in the driveway. She looked up, but the blinds were closed. Her skin went crawly.

She waited. The sound, whatever it was, faded. It couldn't be her parents. Not this early.

She breathed.

She went back to her letters and spelled out her word.

WARNING.

The Specter's moon-white hand flashed in her eyes.

It was only a movie, she thought. *Imaginary. Fictional.*

Outside, gravel crunched. She looked up again.

It must be the neighbors, Ramona thought. *Or someone across the street.*

She added up what score her word—WARNING—would have earned if she'd been playing for real.

Since she'd used all seven of her tiles, she'd get fifty bonus points. And she could put her *W* on a double-letter space. That would bring her score to . . .

Sixty-five points.

Outside, a dog started barking. Ramona's stomach tightened.

"Unreal," she said out loud. She scratched her neck. "Fantastic. Made-up."

Still, she walked to the front door and made sure it was locked.

Keep playing, she told herself as she checked the peephole and saw nothing.

She returned to the table and reached into the felt bag for seven more tiles. She placed them in front of her.

E-R-S-E-T-P-C.

She started thinking.

PEST. She pushed the tiles around.

SEER. REST. TREES.

Then she saw it.

SPECTER.

The seven letters in front of her could spell *SPECTER.*

Outside, the dog barked louder and gravel crunched again, only now the crunching sounded like footsteps. *Steady* footsteps. *Determined* footsteps.

They were too close to be coming from across the street.

The words on the Scrabble board seemed to pulse.

WARNING. SPECTER.

Ramona fingered the edge of the table.

It's a coincidence, she thought. *A happenstance.*

She'd made those words—*WARNING* and *SPECTER*— because *The Specter* was still so fresh in her mind.

She turned back to the Scrabble board. She scooped up all the tiles and dumped them into the felt bag.

All at once, the dog outside stopped barking.

Everything fell quiet.

"Anxious," Ramona said. Her heart pounded in her chest. "Panicky."

The footsteps she'd heard—they could have been the Jeffersons next door.

Couldn't they?

She reached into the felt bag and grabbed seven more tiles.

She spread them in front of her.

E-R-O-N-A-U-Y

There was a creak on the front porch. Ramona held her breath.

Something *scritched* and *scratched* against the front door. It moved back and forth. Back and forth.

"Branches," Ramona whispered. "Twigs." That had to be it. Branches in the wind.

Again, the moon-white skeleton hand flashed in Ramona's mind.

She swallowed.

Play the game, she thought. She looked down at her letters.

YOU. That was an easy one. But she could do better. What did she have left?

E-R-N-A.

EARN.

She shuffled the letters.

The sound at the front door *scritched* and *scratched*.

EARN YOU, she thought. It was two words, and it didn't mean anything. It was nonsense. Rubbish. So everything was fine.

Then, Ramona's mind flickered.

Not EARN, she realized. She shifted the tiles.

NEAR.

NEAR YOU.

Just then, the doorknob jiggled. Ramona saw all her words in her mind.

WARNING.

SPECTER.

NEAR YOU.

The doorknob jiggled again.

Something was happening. She couldn't deny it any-more. Something . . . *awful. Unusual. Terrible.* Quickly, Ramona dumped all the letters into the felt bag.

The game, she thought. It had been warning her. Help-ing her. It would tell her what to do.

Words *always* helped.

There was a thud on the front porch, as if someone had dropped something heavy. Ramona gritted her teeth.

The door rattled, and Ramona reached into the bag and counted out seven tiles. The Scrabble game was on her side. It would protect her.

Moving fast, she slapped the tiles onto the table, straight-ened them, and turned over the ones that were facedown.

A-T-O-E-L-O-T

She shifted them around.

Think, she told herself. The front door rattled again.

Ramona made a word.

TOOL.

That's it, she thought. A *tool.* An *instrument.* A *weapon.* She needed a tool to defend herself, or to wedge the door shut—a wrench, a hammer, something. But what tool exactly?

She looked at her remaining letters.

T-E-A.

Tea. That made no sense.

The front door rattled once more.

She rearranged the last three letters: *EAT, ATE, ETA.*

Hurry, she told herself.

There was a clicking in the doorknob, like someone fiddling with the lock. Inserting a key.

Or a moon-white bone.

Faster, she thought. *Faster!*

It couldn't be *TOOL.* The remaining letters just didn't add up.

Maybe it was *T-O-O?*

TOO.

Too what?

The doorknob turned.

She shifted letters.

Then she saw it.

She froze.

With a creak, the front door opened.

A night breeze blew into the house, but Ramona didn't even turn.

Her eyes were locked on the final seven-letter message.

———

Ramona's parents got home a little before midnight.

When her mother walked into the house, everything was quiet.

Ramona must have gone to bed on time, she thought. *Good girl.*

On her way into the kitchen, she noticed the Scrabble board on the table. She smiled. Ramona loved Scrabble.

But something was off. Everything on the table was crooked. Scrabbled. A kitchen chair was even tipped over, and the Scrabble board, which should have been chock-full of Ramona's words, had only two small words on it.

Only two small words.

TOO LATE.

MY HAND, RIGHT THERE

HAVE you ever seen someone's initials carved into a tree trunk?

I'll bet you have. That kind of thing is practically everywhere. In every city. In every park. In every forest.

Some people think it's sad, the way people carve their names into trees.

But not me.

I think it's stupid.

I mean, carving your name—your actual name—into a tree trunk? That's going to be a pretty big clue when someone decides to start seeking revenge for what you did to their tree.

So I'd never carve my name into a tree trunk. Or even my initials.

I'd carve . . . something else.

In fact, if you promise to keep a secret, I'll tell you something.

You know that jagged lightning bolt carved into the maple tree down by the side of the highway? Or that big eyeball carved into the ash tree over by the middle school? Or that devil's pitchfork carved into the giant oak near the west side of Main Street?

I'm the guy who put those things there.

And those aren't the only markings I've left on trees in this town. Not even close.

I know some people think I shouldn't be carving *anything* into trees. I know they think I'm "hurting them." But give me a break.

Trees can't feel things. They're just . . . trees.

Besides, I *love* seeing my marks all around town and knowing I made them. Carving a tree is like making an announcement to the world that I, Finn Lewis, had been somewhere and done something.

It's like leaving a little piece of myself behind.

That's why I always carry my Swiss Army Knife. So I can leave my marks when the chance comes around. You've seen Swiss Army Knives before, right? They're those red-and-silver pocketknives that have, like, a thousand tools in them. Mine has a large blade, a small blade, a can opener, a corkscrew, a magnifying glass, two screwdrivers, and a wood saw that's sturdy enough to saw through a branch as thick as my wrist.

It's the wood saw that works best for carving, in case you were wondering.

That's also why, one Friday evening last October, I made sure my wood saw was good and sharp. My parents had gone on a dinner date, so I pocketed my knife, left the house, and headed for the Green Springs County Library on the edge of town. Our library's got this long, winding entrance that's lined with massive aspen trees, and I thought that maybe I'd carve a giant skull into one of them. With twisting flames around it if I had time.

It was cold that night. Really cold. Gusts of wind blew, and October leaves hissed. I'd pulled the sleeves of my jacket down over my knuckles to keep my hands warm. But the cold was good, I told myself. The cold meant people would stay home, mostly, and the streets would be empty. It meant I'd be free to carve my skull and my flames as deep as I liked without getting caught.

So I walked. Fallen leaves skittered along the streets, and with each step, I could feel my Swiss Army Knife in my pocket kind of *thumping, thumping, thumping* against my left leg.

Then I reached the library's long, winding entrance.

Where I stopped.

The entrance was blocked off with orange cones and four traffic barricades and long stretches of yellow tape. There was a sign hanging up on one of the traffic barricades. It said:

LIBRARY CLOSED TILL MONDAY AT 10:00 A.M.

NEW SIDEWALKS: WET CEMENT

DO NOT ENTER

Perfect, I thought. *This is perfect.* With the entrance blocked off, I'd have the library's trees all to myself. I could take all the time I wanted to leave my mark.

Then an idea hit me. Like a bolt of lightning.

Ka-zot!

I stared at those words—WET CEMENT.

A picture came into my head. Of cement handprints.

I'd seen them before—wide-fingered handprints in concrete by the grocery store, small handprints in the sidewalks at the elementary school, deep handprints in the walking path down by the park. You've probably seen cement handprints too. They're all over.

Standing there—in front of those barricades and that yellow tape—I felt my skin start to buzz. I realized there were other ways I could leave little pieces of myself behind.

A *cement handprint,* I thought. Sure, lots of people had made them. But I could make mine . . . unique. I could use my Swiss Army Knife to add twisting flames around it.

As soon as I thought this, I knew I had to do it.

I mean, my carvings on trees were one thing. But my handprint. That was like . . . *me.* If I pressed my hand into the cool cement by the Green Springs County Library, every time I'd pass by that place, I'd get to look down and think to myself, *That's my hand, right there.*

For the rest of my life.

My hand. Right there.

A piece of myself left behind.

I took in a quick, cold breath. The leaves in the aspens along the library's long, winding entrance swirled in front of me. I checked up and down the street. The roads were

empty, so I lifted the yellow tape and walked quickly past the massive aspen trees, which swirled and hissed as I passed them by.

The library came into view. Then I saw them—the new sidewalks.

They went around the library, where splotchy grass and dirt used to be. They glistened smooth and wet, and in the early evening light, they gave off a kind of grayish glow.

A dusty, sweet smell hung in the air.

I flexed my hands.

There was no one around. Just me and the trees and the new sidewalks. I shivered, but I took off my jacket and draped it over the branch of a tall aspen nearby.

I didn't want to get wet cement on my sleeves.

I rubbed my arms to keep them warm, and I paced back and forth in front of the new sidewalks. Then I found it.

The perfect spot.

It was a few feet to the left of the front door—not so close that people would step on it, but close enough that most everybody who came to the library would see it.

I knelt down.

My hand. Right there.

Above me, aspen leaves swirled and spun.

I wiped my hand on my pants. I decided to make my handprint first. Then I'd add the twisting flames.

I spread my fingers. The cement smelled like moss and chemicals, and I wondered how many people would see my handprint. How many people visited the Green Springs County Library each day? Was it dozens? Hundreds?

I pressed down.

The cement was cold, like fresh snow. But I pressed hard. I leaned in and made my print deep. The cement gelled between my fingers, and I held my hand there, perfectly still, just to make sure my print would stay when I lifted up.

I waited.

Goose bumps rose on my arms. Suddenly, the wind picked up and the trees hissed louder. Above me, leaves swirled and swirled. Everything seemed to shift, and the cement stiffened and hardened against my skin.

That should do it, I thought. I moved to lift my hand. When I did, nothing happened.

My hand wouldn't budge.

I tried again, not too rough because I wanted my handprint to look neat, not messy.

But I couldn't pull free.

I leaned back. I strained. My hand didn't shift even a bit. I yanked. I groaned. I stopped caring about whether I messed up my handprint or not, and I pulled as hard as I could.

Nothing.

I was stuck.

I got into a squatting position and braced my feet against the ground.

It was no use.

Whatever I tried—jerking, yanking, wrenching—did

nothing. The cement in front of the Green Springs County Library had me. The wind blew. The leaves in the trees swirled and fluttered.

"Come on," I said out loud, and it was so cold I could actually see my breath. I looked at my jacket on the nearby branch.

The cement got harder. The night got colder.

My hand and the sidewalk had become one.

<hr>

It didn't take long before I started yelling.

Sure, I didn't want to get caught with my hand in the cement. But what would you have done, stuck there with no one in sight, shoulders starting to quake from the cold, daylight long gone?

"Somebody!" I hollered, crouched in a squatting position. "Help!"

No one answered. Most likely, no one heard.

Like I said, the library's at the edge of town, at the end of a long, winding entrance.

Plus, there was . . . something else.

Each time I yelled, the aspen trees all around me seemed to rustle and hiss louder. Like they were drowning me out.

I know that sounds crazy.

I hunched in the cold, and I thought about my parents. They'd be getting home from their dinner date soon, and they'd be wondering where I was. They'd call me, but my cell phone was in my jacket pocket, hanging on the nearby branch.

I thought that maybe I could reach it, so I spread myself out as far as I could and kicked at my jacket with one foot. My hope was that somehow I'd hook it with a toe and reel it in.

And maybe it was a trick of the swirling darkness, but every time my foot got close, it seemed like that nearby branch shifted in the nighttime breeze. Like it moved slightly away from me, just out of reach.

Soon, my phone started ringing. I stretched and kicked, but it was no good.

I knew it was Mom and Dad. When I didn't answer, they'd probably start driving around town checking for me at the baseball bleachers, the movie theater, the gas station where I sometimes bought sodas.

They'd never think to check the library. Never. I just wasn't the kind of kid who went there.

Even if they did come to the edge of town, they'd see the library's barricaded entrance, the yellow tape, the WET CEMENT sign, and they'd look for me someplace else.

After a while—maybe an hour, maybe two—my phone stopped ringing. I figured its battery died.

Not long after that, my voice gave out from screaming.

By that time, my hand in the cement had gone completely numb. The skin on my free arm had turned bluish-white. And my ears would not stop prickling.

There was nothing to do but shiver and wait.

Eventually, the moon rose. The night fell silent. It was just swirling leaves and my stuck hand and the bitter cold.

I tried to fall asleep. I thought that I could handle the cold better if I was unconscious. Or at least I thought that sleeping would help the time pass faster. But no matter what I tried—curling into a ball, pulling the neck of my T-shirt up over my head, shifting into a dozen different positions—I couldn't get warm enough to even stop quivering, let alone to drift off to sleep.

At what I figured was around two in the morning, I did some math. The sign at the barricaded entrance said the library would open on Monday at ten a.m.

Fifty-six hours, I figured.

That's how long it would be before anybody showed up to help me.

Fifty-six hours. October hours. Hungry hours. Ice-cold hours.

Already my lips were stinging. Already my toes hurt. Already I was thirsty.

I thought about frostbite. I'd learned about it in health class last year, but I hadn't really been paying attention when we'd talked about it. It had different stages, didn't it? Three of them? Or four?

Was I in one of them already?

I bounced up and down. I rocked back and forth.

Nothing helped.

How long did it take, I wondered, for someone to freeze to death? Twenty hours? Ten? Even less?

I didn't know. But in the darkness, I could practically feel the weight of the aspens' heavy nighttime shadows.

Fifty-six hours, I thought.

———

Some time later, when I couldn't even feel my face, I shifted onto my side and felt a lump in my pocket.

My Swiss Army Knife.

I don't know why I didn't think of it sooner. Maybe because I hadn't been using it to carve into anything. I wrangled it out of my pocket with my free hand and pulled open the large blade with my teeth. Then I brought it down and chopped at the cement, hoping to chip it away.

It didn't work.

I tried hacking, careful not to get too close to my fingers. I tried using other tools—the small blade, the wood saw, even the corkscrew.

Nothing made any difference. It was like my knife was made of plastic. I didn't even make a mark.

I slumped forward and closed my eyes.

I remembered the way the sidewalks had looked when I'd first seen them, with their grayish glow. I remembered the way the trees had drowned out my screaming and the way the nearby branch had shifted whenever I'd kicked for my jacket. I thought of all the things I'd carved into trees around town—the jagged lightning bolt, the devil's pitchfork, the big eyeball.

And I thought of the way the leaves in the aspens all around the Green Springs County Library had swirled and swirled and swirled. All night long.

Then, for the second time that night, an idea hit me. Like a bolt of lightning.

Ka-zot!

The idea was this:

Fate.

That what was happening to me right then at the Green Springs County Library was fate. My fate. I know that sounds strange, but I'm telling you, I felt it inside me like a kind of truth.

I felt another truth too. Deep down.

I'd never survive till Monday.

Never.

Not unless I did something. And I'd need to do it while I still had the strength.

I looked at my knife. I started breathing heavy. I thought.

After a minute, I had it—a way I could free myself. I didn't have to pull myself out of the cement or even chisel through it. There was something else I could do to escape.

Something else I could . . . cut.

And I did have a wood saw, one sturdy enough to saw through a branch as thick as my wrist.

So as the night reached its blackest point and frost began to creep up the library windows, the rustling trees finally stilled.

I swallowed hard.

I opened my wood saw, clenched my jaw, and went to work.

———

Dozens, maybe hundreds of people, visit the Green Springs County Library each day. Most of them, I've noticed, push right past the entrance, completely ignoring what's there. I can't say I blame them. It is pretty ghastly.

There are some people, though, who do stop and look. Like the kids who sometimes dare each other to touch it. Or the dog I saw licking it the other day. I threw a rock at him, but I missed by a mile. I've never been good at throwing left-handed.

You might be wondering if I think it was worth it, pressing my hand into that wet cement and leaving a piece of myself behind.

Honestly, it hasn't been easy. Some things I still haven't figured out, like tying my shoes or writing with the other hand. I haven't even tried carving into any trees since that night.

Honestly, I'm not sure I ever will.

I will tell you this, though.

I do like telling my story. I do like pointing it out to people.

So do me a favor, won't you?

Look there. Just there a few feet to the left of the library's main entrance.

Do you see it?

That's my hand right there.

My hand. Right there.

WAKE UP!

LUNA hadn't had the nightmare in years, hadn't even thought about Jingles the Jester in as long as she could remember.

She'd moved past the nightmare. She'd learned to control her fears.

She'd won.

But then, one night, she burst awake. She sat up in the darkness, shaking. Sweat plastered her clothes to her skin.

Worst of all, she was laughing.

When she realized the high cackling sounds filling the night were coming from her own mouth, her laugh transformed instantly.

Into a high, unwavering scream.

※

It had all started when she was seven years old. She'd had a nightmare. Just a nightmare. But the night after that, she'd had the exact same nightmare. And she'd had it again the night after that.

And she'd kept on having it. Every night, for weeks.

It always started the exact same way—with Luna on a stage. Bright lights shone down on her, and rows and rows of faces in an auditorium stared up.

Where am I? Luna always wondered in the dream. *Why am I here?*

Then, from the other side of the stage, she would come. Jingles. Luna didn't know how she knew the clown's name, but she did.

Jingles the Jester.

She wore skinny tights, one leg yellow and one leg purple, and a yellow-and-purple checkered vest. From across the stage, she would dance slowly toward Luna, taking high-kneed steps, and the bells on her three-pointed hat and the ends of her shoes would rattle. The audience would laugh, a little, and Luna would start to sweat.

When Jingles finally reached her, the thin clown would be so close that Luna could smell her flowery perfume and minty breath. Then Jingles would reach into her checkered vest and pull out a wand.

This was the part of the nightmare that always made Luna twist and squirm beneath her sheets.

Because Jingles the Jester's wand wasn't . . . normal. It had a carved head on the end, an exact miniature of Jingles's own head. It had the same small nose, the same high cheeks, the same white skin, and the same purple lips.

Jingles would raise the wand up, and the carved mouth on the wand would move—not like a puppet's mouth, but like a real person's—and the wand would speak. In a high-pitched, syrupy-sweet voice, the wand would say, "Time for laughter."

Luna would try to back away.

Then Jingles would turn the wand toward the audience, and the talking wand would give a sugary command:

"Laugh!"

And the audience would.

They'd burst into an explosion of laughter, a rupture that would fill the room.

There'd be high laughs, low laughs, snorting laughs, cackling laughs, laughs that tittered, and laughs that hissed. The sound would swell and rise.

I need to get away, Luna would think. She'd turn from side to side. *How do I get away?*

Then, one by one, the faces in the audience would change. The laughers' eyes would widen. They would go from looking delighted to confused to worried to, finally, terrified.

Under the bright theater lights, Luna would know what was happening.

The people in the audience could not stop laughing. No matter how hard they tried. They couldn't stop. And they'd never stop. They'd just keep on laughing and laughing.

Forever.

Then the worst part of the nightmare would come.

The laughter would grow, and Jingles the Jester would smile her thin-lipped smile and point her wand at . . . Luna. The little head would open its mouth and say in its syrupy-sweet voice, "You should be laughing too."

No, Luna would think, and she'd try to run, but it would feel as if her feet were cemented to the stage.

The wand would order her:

"Laugh!"

And without wanting to, she would. She'd burst into a high, piercing laugh. She'd try to fight it. She'd strain and writhe.

But it wouldn't matter.

Her laughter would fill the stage.

A nightmare, she'd think. *I'm having a nightmare.*

So she'd tell herself to wake up.

Wake up! she'd think. *Wake up now!*

And she would. Always. She'd burst awake and sit up in bed.

In the darkness, though, she'd be laughing.

But in less than a second, her laugh would change—as it had a few minutes earlier—into the high, unwavering scream.

⟶ ⟵

Now, sitting up in bed, she slowed her breathing. She counted to ten.

"Jingles the Jester," she whispered, "is not real."

This was how she'd beaten Jingles years ago, back when she was seven. This was how she'd won. She'd said those words over and over, and she'd convinced herself.

Not real. Not real. Not real.

It had taken months, but in time, the nightmare had

faded. She'd started having it every few nights. Then once a week. Then a couple of times a month. And finally, not at all.

It's over, she had thought one day.

And it had been . . . until a few minutes ago.

Now, five years later, here she was—trying to settle herself, trying to calm the rumbling in her chest.

Because Jingles the Jester was back.

Not real.

Luna whispered those words to herself the next morning as she stepped into the shower.

Not real.

And she whispered them again to herself as she started blow-drying her hair.

Every time Jingles's high-kneed dance or thin-lipped smile came into her mind—as she packed her backpack or sat down at the breakfast table or tied her shoes—she would set her jaw and whisper those words.

Not real. Not real. Not real.

Before she left for school, she could already feel herself beating Jingles back.

Probably, she figured, she wouldn't even have the nightmare again. It would be just the one night. Like a fluke.

Then, as her dad was pulling up to the main doors at school, she saw something—a flash of yellow and purple in one of the school's windows. It was the exact same yellow and purple as Jingles's checkered vest and skinny tights and three-pointed hat.

No, she thought.

She pressed her forehead to the car window, but whatever the yellow-and-purple thing had been, it had vanished. It had been there one second and gone the next.

Luna bit a fingernail. The flash had probably been just a reflection from a passing car or a kid on a bike, she told herself. That was all.

She opened the car door and stepped onto the sidewalk.

It's nothing, she thought.

Still, she'd seen it—the exact same yellow and purple as Jingles the Jester's checkered vest and skinny tights and three-pointed hat.

"Not real," she whispered.

Minutes later, she was sitting in her homeroom class, listening to Principal Hodges run through the morning announcements over the PA system.

I can win, she thought as Principal Hodges announced the day's lunch menu—nachos and chef salads. *I can beat Jingles.* After all, she'd done it before. When she'd been just seven years old.

Through the crackling PA system, Principal Hodges cleared his throat and made his final announcement. "This Friday," he said, "all students will meet in the auditorium for a special assembly."

The auditorium, Luna thought.

"We'll watch a performance," Principal Hodges went on, "by a clown who calls herself . . ." He trailed off and Luna heard him shuffling papers. ". . . Ah, here it is. A clown who calls herself Jingles."

Luna's mouth went dry.

A clown who calls herself Jingles.

No, she thought. *Not real.*

There had to be an explanation.

There are probably loads of clowns named Jingles, Luna thought. *Just like there are loads of clowns named Bozo or Curly or Zippo.*

That had to be it.

Besides, she told herself, Principal Hodges had called Jingles a *clown*, not a *jester*, and clowns and jesters were different. Luna picked up her pencil and drummed it on her desk. If the clown coming to her school had been *her* Jingles the Jester, that was the word Principal Hodges would have used.

Jester.

Not *clown*.

So there was nothing to worry about.

Still, in her head, she heard the syrupy-sweet voice of Jingles the Jester's wand.

"Laugh," the voice called. "Laugh."

Luna set her jaw.

For the rest of the day, she refused to even smile.

The nightmare came to her again that night, and the night after that, and the night after that. It played out the same way it always had, with the stage and the audience and the little talking head. In the end, when the wand turned to Luna and she started laughing—high and piercing—she told herself to *Wake up! Wake up now!*

She always did. But night after night, as she sat up in her bed, sweating and laughing, it seemed to take her slightly longer to bring her laughter under control, slightly longer to stop it and transform it into the high, unwavering scream.

On Thursday, one day before the assembly, a poster appeared in the school hallway.

When Luna saw it, she startled and dropped her biology textbook. It showed Jingles the Jester—*her* Jingles the Jester—flashing a thin-lipped smile. She was wearing the skinny tights, one leg yellow and one leg purple, and the checkered vest.

How? Luna thought.

She inched toward the poster.

"Not real," she whispered.

Across the top, the poster said JINGLES THE JESTER in big, bold letters.

Jester. Not *clown.*

Worst of all, the Jingles on the poster held a wand.

It was *the* wand. The one with the little matching head. Luna touched her neck.

"She's real," she whispered, and her heart thudded.

She stared at the poster without blinking. She read the words at the bottom.

MAKING AUDIENCES LAUGH FOR FIVE YEARS
AND COUNTING.

Five years and counting.

Her nightmares had started five years ago.

Luna closed her eyes. In the hallway, it was as if she were dreaming. She saw the stage, the bright lights, the twisting faces of the audience. She saw the exact moment when everyone in the audience realized what was happening to them—when their faces strained and tears formed in their eyes—when they hung perfectly balanced on the too-thin line between a sparkling laugh and an uncontrollable scream.

"Wake up," Luna whispered to herself in the hallway.

She opened her eyes.

———

I can still win, she told herself on Friday morning when she walked into her homeroom class. She didn't have to let Jingles the Jester control her—not the one in her nightmares or the one on the poster.

Besides, she'd found a logical explanation for everything. One that made perfect sense.

Back when she'd been seven, she must have seen Jingles perform somewhere. Maybe Jingles had visited her first-grade class or maybe Luna had simply seen one of Jingles's posters hanging up around town, in a grocery store or someplace

That must have been why her nightmares had started.

Plus, Luna had heard once that everyone you see in your dreams is someone you've also seen in real life—a man on the street, a girl from TV, a clown from a poster. All of them, she'd heard, you've seen before.

It explains everything, Luna thought as she unzipped her jacket and settled into her desk.

So after lunch, when Principal Hodges got on the PA system and dismissed students for the assembly, Luna stood with the rest of her classmates.

She would watch Jingles the Jester's show. She would watch Jingles dance and juggle and maybe even get hit in the face with a pie.

This, she knew, would fix everything. This would prove to her, once and for all, that Jingles was nothing but an ordinary clown.

And she would win. She would beat the nightmare.

Minutes later, she walked into the auditorium.

She took her seat. The auditorium doors closed and the lights dimmed.

She waited.

Finally, Jingles the Jester stepped out from behind a curtain.

Luna's stomach tightened.

Jingles was wearing her tights, one leg yellow and one leg purple, and her yellow-and-purple checkered vest.

I can win, Luna thought. She flexed her neck.

Jingles began her show by doing the ordinary clown things. She juggled five brightly colored balls. She rode a unicycle with a bowling pin balanced on her head. She cut a length of rope that seemed to keep growing longer and longer.

Through it all, Luna didn't smile. Not even once.

Nothing but an ordinary clown, she thought as the assembly wore on.

Then, when the assembly was almost over, Jingles raised one hand and spoke.

"For my final trick," she said, her voice ringing through the auditorium, "I will need a volunteer."

Hands shot into the air.

A vibration rippled through Luna's chest. Jingles walked back and forth across the stage. A few kids called out, "Me! Me!" Others waved their arms.

Then Jingles stopped. Her eyes met Luna's. Her thin-lipped smile widened.

"You," she said, and she pointed. "You're the one I want."

Everyone turned.

Luna didn't move.

"Oh, don't be shy," Jingles said.

"Go on," people whispered, and someone in the row behind Luna nudged her shoulder.

Do it, Luna told herself. If she did, she could end things. If she could stand on that stage and let Jingles do a card trick or a balancing act or a juggling stunt, she could win, once and for all.

She could end the nightmares. Forever.

So slowly, she stood. She walked down the aisle and climbed the five stairs to the stage.

Soon, bright lights shone down on her, and rows and rows of faces stared up.

She clenched her fists.

From across the stage, Jingles started dancing. She took high-kneed steps, and the bells on her hat and the ends of her shoes rattled. The students in the audience laughed, a little, and Luna brought her hands together.

It'll be okay, she told herself.

Then Jingles was there, just by her side, so close that Luna could smell her flowery perfume and minty breath.

Luna tried not to shiver.

Jingles reached into her vest, paused for a second, and pulled out . . . the wand.

Luna stared at its small nose, its high cheeks, its white skin, and its purple lips.

She forced herself to blink.

Jingles raised the wand up. A few people cheered, but Jingles waved her arm and pointed to the small head.

Silence fell.

Then, just like in the nightmare, the wand spoke—not like a puppet, but like a real person.

"Time for laughter," the head said, and the wand's voice came out high and syrupy.

This couldn't be happening.

I need to get away, Luna thought, but her feet seemed cemented to the stage. *How do I get away?*

"Laugh!" the wand commanded the audience.

Please, no, Luna thought.

But her classmates burst into an explosion of laughter. They laughed high and low. They snorted and hissed. Sweat dripped down Luna's face.

Then, one by one, the faces of her classmates changed. They went from delighted to confused to worried to terrified.

The sound of their laughter swelled.

The nightmare, Luna realized. *I'm having the nightmare.*

But what if she wasn't?

Next to her, Jingles the Jester smiled her thin-lipped smile, and slowly, she turned the wand . . . to Luna.

The little head opened its mouth.

Wake up, Luna thought. *Wake up now!*

"You should be laughing too," the wand said.

No, Luna thought.

"Laugh!" the little head commanded.

Wake up, Luna thought again. *Please!*

Without wanting to, she burst into laughter. She fought it, but her laugh came out high and piercing.

It'll be okay, she told herself. Any second now, she would wake up.

She always woke up.

Still, her laughter filled the stage.

Wake up, she told herself again. She pinched her arm until it hurt. Next to her, Jingles the Jester started dancing to her laughter. Real tears spilled onto Luna's cheeks.

Wake up! she ordered herself again. *Wake up!*

Nothing happened.

No matter how many times she commanded, no matter how hard she tried, she stayed on that stage under the bright theater lights.

And she laughed . . . and laughed . . . and laughed.

WE ALL SCREAM FOR ICE CREAM

THE porch thermometer said it was ninety-four degrees. In the shade.

Too hot to play softball. Too hot to ride bikes. Too hot for eating or sleeping or even moving.

So Chloe was sitting, just sitting, in the ninety-four-degree shade of her covered front porch.

Why, she asked herself, *did the piece-of-junk air conditioner have to break this week?*

But Chloe knew why.

It was the same reason she only got called on in history class when she didn't know the answer, the same reason she only spilled chocolate milk on herself when she was wearing her favorite sweater, the same reason she only tripped in the hallway when she was making eye contact with a super-cute boy.

Because the universe was . . . stupid.

Of course the air conditioner had fizzled and died smack-dab in the middle of an August heat wave. When else would it have broken?

Stupid universe, Chloe thought as she shifted in the

porch chair and noticed the sweat marks her hands left on the armrests.

Over the past few days, she'd tried everything she could think of to cool off. She'd taken long, cold showers. She'd read books in front of a blowing fan. She'd sipped cold 7Up while sliding ice cubes over her neck and arms.

But nothing had worked.

"I'd do anything," Chloe said out loud, "to cool off."

Just then, as if in answer, electric chimes rang out over housetops and telephone lines. Chloe tilted her head toward the music—"Pop Goes the Weasel."

She knew what the ringing song meant.

An ice cream truck!

She sat up. Ice cream would feel *sooo* good.

The chiming music grew louder. Then, at the far end of Azalea Street, a white truck, covered in pictures of ice cream scoops the colors of planets, came into view and headed . . . in the completely wrong direction.

Stupid universe, Chloe thought again as the truck pulled away.

She stood up.

I can catch it, she thought. She reached into her shorts pocket and pulled out the five-dollar bill she'd been planning to use for more 7Up from the corner store.

Then, despite the heat, she ran. Her arms pumped. Her

flip-flops barely stayed on her feet. Sweat dripped from her face. After a minute, she was just four houses behind the truck—close enough that the driver might see her. She started waving her five-dollar bill.

"Ice cream!" she yelled, hoping she'd be heard over the chimes. "Hey, ice cream!"

Finally, the truck pulled to the curb. "Pop Goes the Weasel" faded out.

She caught up, panting. She stopped, bent forward, and rested her hands on her knees.

The ice cream man slid open the little window.

"I scream, you scream, we all scream for ice cream," he called out in a high, bright voice. "What can I get you?"

Whoa, Chloe thought. Because this ice cream man looked . . . different. He was young, and he had a round face and bright red cheeks. He wore a paper hat, a white jacket, and a bow tie. A real bow tie.

Breathing hard, Chloe scanned the menu on the side of the truck.

There were three ice cream sizes to choose from—a one-scoop cone, which the menu called the Arctic Chill, a two-scoop cone, which it called the Wintery Blast, and a three-scoop cone, which it called the Nice and Easy Ultra-Freezie.

Strange names, Chloe thought. But if there was any chance of cooling off, especially after chasing an ice cream truck for two whole blocks on the hottest day of the year, it would come, Chloe knew, from the biggest ice cream cone that money could buy.

"I would like," Chloe said, trying to talk and catch her breath at the same time, "the Nice and Easy . . . Ultra-Freezie. . . all chocolate . . . please."

"Three big chocolate scoops coming right up," the ice cream man said, and he flashed a smile. He grabbed a silver ice cream scooper.

Somehow, Chloe noticed, the ice cream man wasn't sweating a bit. Despite the blazing sun and his white jacket and his bow tie, he looked as crisp and chilled as an October morning.

It must be cool in an ice cream truck, Chloe thought. *If it weren't, all the ice cream would melt.*

The ice cream man finished scooping and passed Chloe her cone.

It was perfect, like an ice cream cone from a cartoon, tall and carefully balanced. She took it and held out her five-dollar bill, realizing she hadn't seen any prices on the menu.

"Oh, no, no," the ice cream man said. He waved the money away.

Chloe kept her arm outstretched. The ice cream man smiled once more. His smile was like one from a toothpaste commercial—white-toothed and wide.

He didn't take the money.

"You mean this ice cream is free?" Chloe said. She'd never heard of an ice cream truck giving out free cones before.

"Well," the ice cream man said, and his teeth glistened like pearls. "Let's just say the Nice and Easy Ultra-Freezie doesn't cost money."

With that, he dropped his ice cream scooper into a water-filled bucket, pulled the sliding window closed, and climbed back into the driver's seat.

Strange, Chloe thought again as the ice cream man flipped a switch and "Pop Goes the Weasel" started chiming.

The truck pulled away. Chloe wiped her forehead. The backs of her knees felt gummy and sticky. Damp hair clung to her neck.

She eyed the ice cream cone that didn't "cost money."

Who was that man? Chloe wondered. Did he really drive around town giving out free treats to kids on the hottest day of the year? Was he really just a cheerful ice cream truck driver?

Chloe squinted at the Nice and Easy Ultra-Freezie.

Chocolate drips began to trickle down her fingers. If she didn't eat soon, her ice cream would be nothing but a sticky puddle and she'd have sprinted in the summer heat for nothing.

She listened to the fading sounds of "Pop Goes the

Weasel." She felt the sun beating down on her arms and face.

She lifted the cone to her mouth.

Then, with the tip of her tongue, she licked it. Just a little.

At once, she knew she'd made the right choice. The ice cream was sweet and cold, and even that one taste made Chloe feel slightly less sweaty.

She licked again, and her neck seemed suddenly less slick.

She walked home and she ate, and little by little, she felt cooler.

The sun blazed in the sky, but somehow, the Nice and Easy Ultra-Freezie even made the backs of her knees seem less sticky. She swallowed chocolatey gulp after chocolatey gulp, and a coolness seemed to spread through her entire body.

By the time she returned to her chair on the front porch, the sweat on her face had dried completely. Even her hair felt light and airy and dry.

We all scream for ice cream, she thought.

The ice cream had worked when nothing else had—not cold showers or 7Up or ice cubes.

She bit into another creamy glob, and even though the porch thermometer rose to ninety-five—in the shade—a cool chill ran down her neck.

The Nice and Easy Ultra-Freezie had done it!

Maybe, she thought, *the universe isn't so stupid after all.*

Because here she was. Eating ice cream. Smack-dab in the middle of an August heat wave.

And it didn't cost her a thing.

✦

The effects of the Nice and Easy Ultra-Freezie lasted for the rest of the day. While Chloe's mother practically melted in front of a blowing fan, Chloe felt comfortable and cool.

The next morning, when Chloe woke up, she even found that she'd crawled under her covers during the night.

She couldn't believe it. Ever since the air conditioner had broken, she'd had to sleep on top of her covers—not under them—and she'd woken up again and again in the night, way too hot to stay comfortable.

But the day after eating the Nice and Easy Ultra-Freezie, she woke tucked comfortably under three layers—a sheet, a blanket, and a bedspread.

She got up and took a warm shower. She dressed in long pants and made herself a hot breakfast—scrambled eggs and sausage.

"You're wearing jeans?" her mom asked when she came into the kitchen. She was in an old tank top and loose shorts, and she was rolling a frozen water bottle back and forth across her forehead. "It's supposed to be one hundred and four today."

Chloe shrugged. "I'll change later if it gets too hot."

But it didn't get too hot. Not for Chloe.

The whole day, she felt fine. She didn't sweat, and she didn't need ice or 7Up or anything else.

When the sun went down, she even pulled on a jacket because a light breeze picked up and chilled her skin.

―⁓―

A week later, the heat wave was still going on.

But not for Chloe.

She couldn't understand it. Despite the blistering summer sun and the record temperatures, she wore long sleeves during the day and sweatshirts at night.

Finally, September came.

That was when the new air conditioner arrived.

Chloe felt the change when she stepped into the house after school one afternoon. She opened the front door, and a wall of cold air hit her.

In the entryway, she dropped her backpack.

"Whoa," she said to her mom, who was somehow wearing a flowing skirt and a thin blouse. "It's pretty cold in here."

"Yeah," her mom said. "Isn't it great?"

Chloe didn't answer.

After a few minutes, her fingertips and the end of her nose felt chilled. She pulled on a hoodie and wrapped herself in a blanket before sitting down to do her history homework.

A few hours later, she couldn't take it anymore. When

her mom wasn't looking, she darted into the hallway to bump up the temperature on the thermostat.

Standing in front of it, something wasn't right.

She'd expected the thermostat to be set low—to sixty-six or sixty-eight degrees, at the most. She'd figured her mom, sick of the sweltering heat, had overdone things and blasted the new air conditioner way too hard.

But the thermostat was set at seventy-eight degrees. Barely even cool.

In the hallway, Chloe hunched her shoulders and hugged herself. She blinked, tapped the thermostat, and checked it again.

It didn't change.

How could that be?

For hours, Chloe had been adjusting the blanket around her shoulders and rubbing her hands together to keep them warm.

And all the while, it had been seventy-eight degrees.

A "comfortable" seventy-eight degrees.

———✦———

After that, no matter what Chloe did, she was always just a little bit cold.

Nothing seemed to warm her up. Not sitting in front of the space heater she'd dug out of the closet. Not blow-drying her hair for far longer than she needed to. Not even soaking in a steaming bath. No matter how hard she tried, she couldn't get all the way warm.

The Nice and Easy Ultra-Freezie, she thought one day as she sat on a blowing heat vent.

She shook her head. That had been weeks ago.

Then, on a bright October day, Chloe started shivering.

She couldn't help it. She was walking home from school, and all at once, her shoulders started shaking. The shaking spread to her neck and her arms and her fingers. She put her hands together and blew on them.

Stupid universe, she thought.

"Are you feeling all right?" her mom asked when she saw Chloe that night, huddled with her arms tight around her, snuggled under three blankets. "Do you have a fever?" She crossed the room and placed a hand on Chloe's forehead.

"I'm not sick," Chloe said, and her words came out shaky. "I'm just really cold."

She remembered the words of the ice cream man.

"The Nice and Easy Ultra-Freezie doesn't cost money," he'd said as he'd flashed his toothpaste-commercial smile.

Thinking of that smile made Chloe shiver even more.

———

By November, her teeth had started chattering. She couldn't make them stop. They clacked quietly as she sat in her classes, and sometimes, students around her would turn and stare.

Her mother took her to the doctor.

The first thing he did was take her temperature.

It was 98.6 degrees. Normal.

He checked her pulse and asked if she'd been experiencing any tingling. *No.* Any aches. *No.* Any muscle cramps. *No.* He asked about her diet, her exercise habits, her sleep patterns. He talked to her about anxiety and stress.

He asked if anything out of the ordinary had happened in her life recently.

She thought of the ice cream man and the Nice and Easy Ultra-Freezie but she didn't say anything.

"You don't seem to have an infection," the doctor finally said, tapping his pen on his clipboard. "And you're not hurt. You just seem to be really cold."

Chloe tried to nod, but her shivering made it too hard.

The doctor turned to Chloe's mom. "This is a bit of a mystery," he said. "I've never seen anything like it. For now, try to keep her warm. Blankets. Hot baths. Soup. That kind of thing." He spoke calmly, as if everything would, of course, be all right. "In time, this will probably go away on its own."

He turned back to Chloe.

"It was probably just something you ate."

❧ ❧

December came, and so did the first snow.

Chloe could barely speak through her chattering teeth and quivering lips. Her toes had gone completely numb, and she couldn't even wiggle them anymore.

She listened, all the time, for the ice cream truck—the fast-chiming "Pop Goes the Weasel." Her hope was that she could somehow find it and pay the driver for the Nice and Easy Ultra-Freezie with money instead of whatever *this* was.

But it was December.

All the ice cream trucks had gone away.

In their place, hot chocolate huts had popped up. Chloe trudged past one called the Warming Shack on her walk to school one morning. It was snowing, and Chloe pulled her hat down low over her ears even though she knew it wouldn't make any difference.

Stupid universe, she thought as she walked.

She peered into the Warming Shack. Inside, a plump, red-cheeked woman busied herself boiling water and stirring powder and spraying whipped cream onto cups of cocoa.

Chloe shuffled close. The woman looked like a cheery grandmother, like she'd brought her hot chocolate down personally from the North Pole. She wore a colorful sweater and shining earrings and a frilly apron.

The Warming Shack, Chloe thought.

Just then, the woman looked up and pulled open the little sliding window.

"Oh, you poor thing," she said. "You must be absolutely freezing."

Chloe tried to nod.

"Well, take this." The woman held out a tall cup of cocoa.

Steam rose from it. Chloe took it between her quivering hands.

Hot chocolate, she thought. *Oh, please let this work.*

She'd tried everything else. Blankets and baths. Heaters and hot pads.

The woman in the shack nodded. "Go on," she said. "Drink up."

Chloe lifted the cup and sipped.

Suddenly, she felt . . .

Warmth.

Actual warmth.

It started in her mouth the second she tasted the sugary chocolate.

Her eyes widened.

Her teeth had stopped chattering.

She couldn't believe it.

Her teeth had stopped chattering!

She sipped again, and the warmth spread from her mouth to her stomach. It swelled inside her like an inflating balloon.

"Oh," Chloe said when her quivering hands slowed and stilled. She looked from the steaming cup to the woman in the shack. "Oh, thank you."

She was warm! For the first time in months. Her ears. Her fingers. Her face. All warm!

Tears welled in her eyes.

Chloe took another sip—a big one this time. A gulp, really. The woman in the Warming Shack smiled. Her smile was white-toothed and wide—like one from a toothpaste commercial.

Chloe unzipped her coat.

She reached into her pocket and pulled out a five-dollar bill.

"What do I owe you?" she said.

"Oh, no, no." The woman pointed at the steaming cup, more than half drunk now. "You don't understand."

Chloe stopped.

"My hot chocolate doesn't cost money," the woman said. She smiled again, and her teeth glistened like falling snow.

Sweat built up on Chloe's forehead.

Her hands started to shake, but not from the cold.

Slowly, she turned to the menu beside the sliding window. She read the words that were printed across the top:

TODAY'S SPECIAL: THE SMOOTH AND SWEETER

MEGA-HEATER.

Her mouth fell open. The heat inside her rose. She peeled off her coat.

It didn't help. Sweat began to drip down her face.

Stupid universe, she thought.

Stupid, stupid universe.

ONE of A KIND

CLONES. That's what it sometimes felt like the twenty-two other students in my sixth-grade art class were.

Middle school clones.

I mean, they all wore the same brand of blue jeans. They all listened to the same pop music. They all spent their weekends at the exact same movie theater downtown.

They all even drew the same things whenever Ms. Beckett gave us an art project to complete. Like the time she assigned us to draw landscapes.

Every one of my classmates—every single one of them—drew a mountain range. With a setting sun behind it and birds fluttering in the sky.

But not me.

I drew a volcano. An erupting one, with lots of smoke and ash and rivers of lava.

When I was working on it, shading in a giant plume of smoke, I caught my desk partner, Olivia Delgado, squinting at it.

"Volcanoes are a part of the landscape too, you know," I told her.

I added a few smoke lines, and Olivia went back to her mountain range.

That's when Ms. Beckett stopped by my desk.

"What do we have here, Emma?" she said.

"My name is Sapphire now," I reminded her as I fingered my earrings. I'd just gotten them—two in my left ear and one in my right.

"Sapphire," Ms. Beckett repeated with a nod. "I'm sorry. I keep forgetting."

"It's okay," I said.

And it really was.

I couldn't blame Ms. Beckett. Officially, my name on the school roster was Emma Davis. The problem was that there were, like, twelve other Emmas in my school. Emma Campbell. Emma Perkins. Emma Green. The list went on.

So I was working to become someone else.

Besides, I liked Ms. Beckett. I liked that she called us future artists. I liked that she decorated her classroom with bright yellow paint and wore her hair in one long braid. I liked that she'd never commented on my new style—not my shiny nail polish or my high boots or my earrings. She was just letting me figure out . . . me.

"Wow," Ms. Beckett said, looking at my volcano. She ran a finger along one of the rivers of lava. "This is . . . good. Really good." She leaned closer. "Excellent shading. Spot-on perspective. Your artistic choices are so . . . unique."

It was that last word that made me smile.

Unique.

That's what the new me, Sapphire Davis, was all about.

The old me, Emma Davis, had been, if I'm being brutally honest here, a bit of a middle school clone. She'd worn blue jeans and listened to pop music and spent her weekends at the movie theater downtown.

But Sapphire Davis. She was going to be something else. She was going to be an original. An artist.

One of a kind.

—❦—

Ms. Beckett gave me an A on my volcano—a 99 percent, which was the highest grade she gave because she said no piece of art was perfect.

She even hung my volcano on the class bulletin board for everyone to see. Then she gave us a new assignment.

"For the next week, my future artists," she said, tossing her long braid over one shoulder, "your assignment will be to draw an animal. Any animal you want."

I fiddled with my three earrings.

The other students would draw, I guessed, birds. That's what Emma Davis would have drawn, anyway. She'd have drawn a soaring eagle or a gliding hawk.

As everyone else pulled out papers and pencils and got to work, I waited. When my classmates were deep into their drawings, I stood and walked to the pencil sharpener. I peered over everyone's shoulders as I went.

Sure enough, Olivia Delgado, my desk partner, was drawing a falcon.

Emma Green was working on a seagull.

Dylan Johnson, who sat by the window, was putting a long beak on a hummingbird.

At the pencil sharpener, I thought.

What would a true original like Sapphire Davis draw?

Just then, a fat spider flitted up the wall. I jumped back. Everyone was so busy working on their drawings that no one saw the spider but me.

No one but me.

So I had it.

An idea for an art project that would truly be one of a kind.

— ⁓ —

I decided to draw not one spider, but three of them. Like my earrings. Everyone else was drawing just one animal, right in the middle of their papers.

I could be different though.

I could put my spiders all around my paper. One up at the top, one near the edge, and one in a low corner.

I made my spiders big—larger than quarters. I drew them hanging in a thin web. I spent hours looking at spider pictures on my phone, and it took me days to sketch out their strange eyes and their tiny, crooked legs and their sharp, curved pincers. Eventually, I thought my spiders were looking pretty good.

At the end of the week, I tapped my boots on the floor. I leaned back in my chair and peered at my drawing.

"Creepy," said Olivia Delgado. She might have scowled.

"Something's still missing," I said.

Behind me, Ms. Beckett spoke.

"What have you been working on this week, Emma?"

"It's Sapphire," I told her.

"Sapphire." She tapped her forehead with a finger as if she were trying to get my name in there. I hoped she would.

I just had to keep acting like Sapphire Davis, keep dressing like her, keep drawing like her, and in time, people would forget about Emma Davis, the middle school clone.

I slid my drawing to the edge of my desk.

"Ooh, spiders," Ms. Beckett said, and she sounded excited. "I've never had a student draw spiders before."

One of a kind, I thought.

"They're not finished," I said, waving a hand at my paper. I had rings on three of my fingers. "They need something. I'm not sure what."

Ms. Beckett squinted and ran a hand down her long braid.

"Ahh," she said. She took my pencil. "What about this?" She added a few small hairs to one of the spiders' legs. The hairs were so thin, so fine, they were almost invisible.

But the spider at the top of my paper seemed to wriggle and squirm.

Wow, I thought.

"It's the details," Ms. Beckett said, "that bring a drawing to life."

I nodded.

She handed the pencil back to me. "Give it a try," she said. "My future artist."

I leaned in. I added the thinnest, finest hairs to one of my spiders' legs, the one near the bottom of my paper, in the low corner.

It worked. I ran my hand over my drawing, and I could practically feel the spiders' hairy bodies.

The bell rang. Before heading to social studies, I took my drawing to my locker. I carried it in my hands, not in my backpack, because I didn't want to crinkle it. I grabbed the dial lock and entered my combination—13-31-13. I'd changed it the same day I'd chosen the name Sapphire.

I reached up and put my drawing on the top shelf and closed my locker with a *click*.

When school ended, I headed back to my locker to get my drawing. As I got close to it, I slowed my walk.

I sensed something in the hallway.

It was a kind of creeping feeling. A skittering on my skin and in the air and everywhere. I got this picture in my head of thin webs, flitting legs, and pinching pincers.

My *spiders*, I thought.

I stepped close to my locker. A coldness seemed to wash over me, like stepping through a web. I reached for the dial to enter my combination, and the creeping feeling swelled.

I jerked my hand away from my locker.

I remembered what Ms. Beckett had said.

It's the details that bring a drawing to life.

A glimmer of an idea rose up in my mind.

No, I told myself. It was too strange. Too impossible.

I entered my combination, 13-31-13. I reached for the metal latch and opened the door.

I jumped back.

There were spiders in my locker. Three of them—bigger than quarters. They were hanging on a thin web just below my coat hook. Their legs flitted, and they headed for the open door.

I backed away.

I could see their strange eyes and their tiny, crooked legs and their sharp, curved pincers. They crept around the locker door. They scuttled their way up the wall.

I fiddled with my earrings.

How had this happened?

The glimmer of the idea I'd had before rose up again, but I forced it down.

The spiders had probably crawled in through the small slits in the locker door. Maybe they'd seen my drawing as I'd carried it down the hall and thought my spiders were real.

Still, I reached one hand into my locker, and I snatched my drawing off the top shelf.

Before looking at it, I tucked my hair behind my ears.

I took in a breath and lifted it up.

My three spiders were still there, right where I'd left them. One was up at the top of the page, another was near the edge, and the last one was in the low corner.

I sighed.

Everything was fine.

———

That night, I sat on my bed and I thought about my spiders. Not the ones in my locker. The ones I'd drawn. I thought about what Ms. Beckett had said when she'd seen my drawing.

"I've never had a student draw spiders before."

Remembering that made a warm bubble fill my chest.

I was becoming Sapphire.

What other animals, I wondered, *would a one-of-a-kind artist draw?*

Not cats or dogs, obviously. Nothing cute either. Not rabbits. Not horses. Not deer.

What about scorpions? I thought. *Or earthworms? Or eels?*

I took out a sketchpad and a pencil. A quiet buzz filled my room. I looked up. There was a moth, darting around my light.

A moth, I thought. I'd have bet anything Ms. Beckett had never seen a student draw a moth before.

So when my bedroom moth finally settled and landed on the wall next to me, I turned to a fresh sheet of paper.

I started drawing.

The moth on my wall was covered in tiny speckles. Its shape was different than a butterfly's. It was narrower and longer, and it had thin antennae. Emma Davis, the old me, had drawn dozens of butterflies.

But this was different.

Look harder, I told myself.

It was the details, Ms. Beckett had said, that brought a drawing to life.

I squinted. The moth's wings were frayed at the ends, like they'd worn out over time.

I drew them that way.

The moth stayed right on my wall and held absolutely still. Like it was posing for me.

After more than an hour, I had it. A perfect moth, complete with all the details.

I signed my name—my new name—at the bottom of the page.

Sapphire Davis.

The next morning, before school started, I put my sketchpad in my locker.

After lunch, I went to get it before art class. I wanted to show my moth to Ms. Beckett, to hear her tell me she'd never had a student draw anything like it before.

When I got to my locker, I slowed.

Again, I sensed something.

Like with the spiders.

Only this time it was different. The feeling inside me was a fluttering, a darting. I got a picture in my head of thin antennae and fraying wings.

My moth, I thought. I grabbed the dial and entered my

combination. 13-31-13. The second I cracked my locker door, a moth darted out.

It fluttered past my face. It flitted down the hallway. Other kids saw it too. Some of them pointed. Dylan Johnson jumped and tried to catch it.

I watched it zigzag down the hall until it turned a corner. A lump rose in my throat.

The idea from the day before came back.

No, I thought. *Spiders and moths are everywhere*. They got into places like art rooms and bedrooms and school lockers. It was what insects did.

So I grabbed my sketchbook and I headed to art class.

— ~ —

That day, Ms. Beckett announced our final project.

"For the next week," she said, "you will draw a self-portrait."

A *self-portrait*, I thought. The fluorescent lights in the art room seemed to hum louder.

I thought of the spiders and the moth in my locker.

"Your self-portrait," Ms. Beckett went on, "should be something that's completely unique, something that only you can make, something that captures your . . . essence."

I fiddled with my earrings.

My essence, I thought.

I put the spiders, the moth, and my locker out of my mind and I drew.

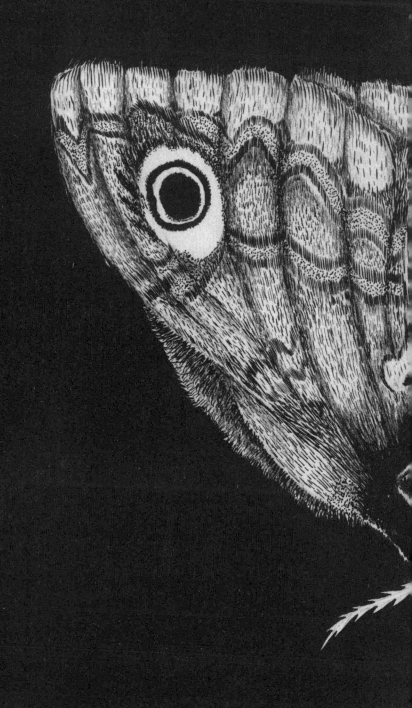

Over the next few days, the other students—Olivia Delgado and Emma Green and Dylan Johnson—drew just their faces, up close, like in a school picture.

But I did something different.

I drew my whole body—my high boots, my shining fingernails, my dark hoodie. I drew myself standing to one side of my paper.

Finally, at the end of the week, I raised my hand and showed my self-portrait to Ms. Beckett.

"I think I'm finished," I said.

Beside my desk, she looked back and forth from the drawing to me.

"It's wonderful," she said. "Such an exact likeness." She squinted. "There's just one detail missing."

She touched her ears.

My earrings, I thought. Somehow, I'd forgotten them.

I nodded. A spark seemed to run from my ears to my fingers. I gripped my pencil. In the exact spots where they should have been, I added three earrings, the final details.

"There you are," said Ms. Beckett, looking over my shoulder. "There's Sapphire. The future artist."

I couldn't help but smile.

Ms. Beckett had called me Sapphire.

I'd done it. I wasn't Emma Davis anymore.

There I was, the new me, right on the page. My shining fingernails. My high boots. My three earrings.

I was one of a kind.

When the bell rang, I carried my self-portrait to my locker.

I thought about the skittering spiders and the fluttering moth. The idea that had kept rising, rising, rising like smoke from a volcano surfaced again.

But I pushed it down. I opened my locker. I took my self-portrait, and I set it on the top shelf.

Don't close the door, a voice inside me said. *Take your drawing and rip it up. Tear it to shreds. Do it now.*

I shook my head. The self-portrait was the best thing I'd ever drawn. I'd gotten all the details right.

I'd captured my . . . essence.

I closed the door.

— ~

When I returned to my locker at the end of the day, I slowed my walk.

Outside my locker, I felt nothing.

Not the creeping, skittering of spiders. Not the fluttering, darting of a moth.

I felt only myself.

So I reached for the dial and entered my combination. 13-31-13.

When I opened the door, my eyes widened. I brought my hands to my mouth.

There she was. Standing in my locker with her eyes closed. She had shining fingernails, high boots, and a dark hoodie.

"What . . ." I muttered.

I moved to slam the door, but she opened her eyes. It was like she was waking up for the first time. She smiled and turned her head from side to side.

A *twin*, I thought.

But no. This thing in my locker was not a twin. It was something else.

A *clone*.

A *middle school clone*.

She looked at me. She stepped out of the locker. She reached up and fiddled with her earrings. She had three of them—two in her left ear and one in her right.

Two of a kind, I thought.

And then, she spoke.

"I'm Emma," she said. A slow crawl swept down the backs of my legs. "But you can call me Sapphire."

ONE MORE PIECE

YES, I broke the doll on purpose.

And I still think it was the logical thing to do.

For my whole life—all twelve years of it—there'd been this doll on the mantel in my living room. A fancy doll. Froofy blue dress. You know the kind. It had a big ceramic head and painted-on eyes and painted-on ears and even painted-on hair.

The problem was that every time I went in the living room that doll seemed to be looking at me. It didn't matter where I was—on the couch, by the door, near the window.

It was like the doll's eyes were staring me down.

Always.

When I was younger, I wouldn't even go into our living room because of that . . . *thing*.

I know that doesn't make any sense, but I'd be reading a book on the living room couch, and suddenly, I'd get the feeling that something was watching me. Or I'd step through the front door at the end of a school day, and out of nowhere, a cold shudder would hit me—on my neck and arms and everywhere. Or I'd be tying my shoes on my way to play basketball at a friend's house, and just like that, my skin would go shivery.

I tried to ignore the doll. I reminded myself that I believed in reason and evidence. After all, I was the vice president of Lab Rats, my middle school science club. Despite the constant shudders and shivers, I knew there was no way a stupid doll could be staring at me.

For some reason, though, seeing her on the mantel always made me stop and straighten my back.

I couldn't understand it.

Then, one day, about two months ago, I came home from an after-school Lab Rats meeting, and I dropped my backpack by the front door. Before I even looked up, that familiar shudder hit me—on my neck and my arms and everywhere.

It's her, I thought. I checked the mantel. Sure enough, the doll's painted-on eyes seemed to be boring into me.

I took two uneasy steps into the living room.

Why, I wondered, *do we even own that stupid doll?*

I realized I didn't know. I rubbed the back of my neck and thought.

Whatever the answer was, I was sure it had something to do with Mom. She loved spooky stuff. Non–science-y stuff. Stuff like monsters and horror movies and creepy pranks. That probably explained how the doll ended up on our mantel in the first place.

But twelve years is a long time to keep *anything* on a shelf. There had to be more to the doll's story than that. Like, where had she come from? What was so important about her that made Mom choose to keep her for so long?

Why was she so special?

At dinner that night, I pushed my last few peas and carrots around my plate, and I asked my parents.

"What's up with . . . her?" I said, and I tilted my head toward the living room.

Dad looked over his shoulder. "Oh, you mean the doll?"

I nodded.

"She's great, right?" Mom said with a smile. "Super creepy."

I put down my fork.

"I'm serious," I said. "Where did she come from?"

Dad scooped a forkful of mashed potatoes. "I think she was a present from your great-aunt Melinda," he said. "She stayed with us for a few days after you were born. When she left, the doll was there. I'd always figured Melinda left her as a gift."

"As a gift," I said.

The doll's head seemed to tilt slightly toward us, like she was eavesdropping.

"Yeah," Dad said. "As a gift for your mom because she's so into . . . you know . . . that kind of stuff."

Dad meant spooky stuff.

Mom looked up from her plate.

"Hang on," she said. "I thought the doll showed up on the mantel way before Aunt Melinda's visit." She tipped her glass of water at Dad. "I thought you put her up there when we decorated the living room."

"Uh . . . no." Dad shook his head. "I don't think so."

I scratched the side of my face. Mom and Dad looked at each other and shrugged.

"I guess we can't remember. Sorry, Mitchell," Mom said.

"You can't remember getting something like . . . that?" I leaned back in my chair. I folded my arms.

I couldn't believe it.

All this time I'd been putting up with that *thing* because I'd thought the doll was special. It would have been fine dealing with her if Mom had told me that my great-great-grandmother had carried the doll on a ship that sailed to America a zillion years ago, or that one of my great-grandfathers had painted her in a village workshop.

But no.

The doll was just a stupid doll—one of those things that ends up on a mantel because there's nowhere else to put it. My parents couldn't even remember where it had come from.

So there was no logical reason for us to keep the doll.

Not even for one more day.

"Ooh." Mom's eyes suddenly went bright and she lowered her voice. "What if the doll walked in here . . . all on her own?" She made a creepy face and waved her hands in front of her.

"She didn't," I said.

After dinner, I went straight to the living room.

I checked the kitchen. My parents were chatting and doing the dishes.

I stepped up to the mantel.

What bothered me the most about the doll, I decided, were her eyes. They were green and small and too realistic. In the middle of her eggshell face, they gave her a fake-looking, way-too-innocent expression.

I'd never touched the doll before. Not once. But it was time to get rid of her, so I shook out my fingers, checked the kitchen again, and grabbed her around the waist.

She was light. Hollow, I figured.

My plan was to head for the garage and hide her in a box or maybe even dump her into the trash.

I took two steps before I stopped.

Think, I told myself. *Be logical about this.*

Mom or Dad would notice if the doll suddenly vanished. Especially since we'd just been talking about her. Then they'd ask me about her, and Mom—the undying lover of all things horrid and creepy—would make me dig her out from where I'd stashed her and bring her back.

If I was going to get rid of the doll—*really* get rid of the doll—I needed a more permanent solution.

An idea crept into my mind.

Slowly, I turned the doll upside down. The floor in our living room was made of hard oak planks. I looked at them and shuffled my feet.

Maybe I shouldn't, I thought. *Maybe I should put the doll back on the mantel and walk away.*

I looked at the doll's eyes. The cold shudder I'd felt a thousand times before hit me—on my neck and arms and everywhere. I reminded myself that this doll wasn't special.

I held her out.

Then I let her slip right out of my fingers.

She fell headfirst. I watched as she went down and down and . . .

Smash!

Like the Big Bang.

She hit the oak floor face-first, and I know this sounds terrible, but nothing has ever sounded more satisfying than that doll's head shattering into dozens of pieces. Porcelain shards scattered across the floor. A bit of her cheek shot over by the window, a slice of her forehead spun close to the sofa, and a single too-realistic eye skittered its way under the recliner.

Problem solved, I thought.

All at once, Mom was behind me.

"Mitchell," she said, staring at the shards on the floor. "What did you do?"

"She—she slipped," I stammered.

It should have been no big deal. I mean, my parents couldn't even remember how they'd gotten the doll in the first place.

But like I said, Mom loved spooky stuff.

She looked at the doll's headless body and the shards scattered on the floor.

"Oh, the poor thing," she said.

She got out the broom and the dustpan and started sweeping.

"You should be more careful, Mitchell," Dad said when he walked in. He knelt by the dustpan and began picking pieces out of it and dropping them into one of those clear plastic baggies. I couldn't believe what was happening.

They were saving the shards!

They were going to try to glue the doll back together.

There had to be dozens of pieces scattered across the living room floor, some of them no bigger than a fingernail clipping.

And this doll was just a stupid doll!

"Look around, Mitchell," Mom said. "Get down on the floor and make sure we've got all the pieces."

I started to tell Mom that putting the doll back together would be impossible, like undoing an explosion, but she reached for the doll's headless body and made a face.

I got down on the floor. I found two pieces along one wall, enough to satisfy Mom, and I dropped them into the baggie. Then I quit looking because there didn't seem to be any point.

The doll was destroyed. Permanently.

Finally, Mom zipped the baggie, cradled the headless dress, and carried everything off.

I'll tell you the truth:

I didn't feel guilty. Not a bit.

I'd done a perfectly logical thing. I'd wanted the doll gone. I'd wanted the cold shuddery feelings to stop.

So I'd dropped her.

It was that simple.

I was glad she was gone forever, and I was certain she was.

Because sure, Mom might try to put her back together again, but there was no way she could do it. The doll was too shattered. Too broken. Fixing her would take too many hours.

So she was finally—*finally!*—out of my life.

⋙⋘

That night, I heard a shuffling, like tiny feet dragging themselves across my bedroom floor. I told myself it was just regular nighttime sounds, and I rolled over and pulled my covers up to my chin.

Later, though, as the sun brightened my room and I opened my eyes, guess what was sitting on the other side of my pillow, not even ten inches from my head?

Her.

She was sitting there, headless, just a frilly blue dress and a jagged porcelain neck. In her lap, she held the baggie, the one with the broken pieces.

I sat up, my heart racing.

I let out a sleepy-throated scream.

That's when Mom burst into my room.

"Mitchell," she said. "What is it?"

Something clicked in my brain.

Mom, I thought. *Of course.*

A few weeks earlier, she'd put a rubber snake in my bathroom sink as a joke. Another time, she'd hid in my closet for more than twenty minutes just so she could jump out when I least expected it.

It was obvious. Mom had done this.

She'd even been the last person I'd seen with the doll.

She must have tiptoed into my room and propped the doll on my pillow as a joke or a punishment for my having broken her in the first place.

Ha ha, Mom, I thought as my heart rate returned to normal.

I wouldn't let her see me startle or flip out though. That was the best way to deal with Mom's pranks. To pretend she hadn't gotten to me.

I stretched and covered the doll with my blankets.

"You screamed," Mom said, actually sounding worried.

I raised my eyebrows. "Who, me?"

"I heard you," Mom said taking a step closer. "Is everything okay?"

"Everything's fine," I said. "Everything's great."

She shook her head. She was probably annoyed her joke wasn't working.

"Well, I'm glad you're okay," she said, and she left.

I peeled back the blanket.

The doll was nothing but a froofy blue dress and a jagged, broken neckline that zigged and zagged. She still had the baggie—the shards of her broken head—on her lap.

On one of those shards, I saw an eye.

It was green and too realistic.

Seeing it made a familiar shudder run over my skin—on my neck and my arms and everywhere.

⌒ ⌒

I left the doll on my pillow when I went to school.

I tried not to think about her, but I saw the jagged line of her neck on the backs of my eyelids every time I blinked.

When the bell rang at the start of chemistry class, Mr. Kunz wrote the words CHEMICAL BONDING on the chalkboard. He launched into a lecture on the ways that atoms become joined to one another, sometimes forever. I tried to pay attention, but I heard a few kids whispering.

"What the heck?" said Jaylen Jones.

"Yikes," said Mikey Simmons.

"That is not okay," said Mia Lopez, the president of Lab Rats.

I turned to see what the whispering was about, and my whole body froze.

There she was.

She was sitting on top of a bookshelf along one side of the classroom. Her baggie, with the shards of her shattered head, was, once again, in her lap.

My Adam's apple seemed to double in size.

How had she gotten here?

Logically, it made no sense. Mom, I knew, wouldn't have done this. Sure, she loved her pranks, but she'd never taken a joke into my school before.

Hannah Wilson raised her hand.

"Mr. Kunz," she said. "I'm sorry, but I'm having a hard time paying attention because of . . . that."

She pointed at the doll.

"Whoa," Mr. Kunz said. "Who put that there?"

Nobody said anything. I looked down at my notebook.

A chatter broke out in the class. I heard words like *freaky*, *creepy*, and even *evil*.

"I asked who put that there," Mr. Kunz said again, and he walked toward the doll. "Whoever did this, you're not in trouble," he said, looking at the snickering boys in the back row. "I like a good joke as much as anyone, but we need to put this thing away so we can focus."

He waited.

The wall clock ticked. I got the sense that the doll was waiting for me to say something. My skin went clammy.

"It was me, Mr. Kunz," I said. Everyone turned. The boys in the back row snickered again. "It was a dumb joke."

"Really, Mitchell?" whispered Mia Lopez.

"Well, come get it." Mr. Kunz waved an arm at me. It didn't seem like he wanted to touch the doll himself. "Put it in your backpack so we can focus."

I nodded and stood up. Everyone watched as I grabbed the doll and her baggie. I zipped her into my backpack and tried to focus on the lesson, but I couldn't stop staring at the two words Mr. Kunz had written on the chalkboard.

CHEMICAL BONDING.

On the floor, my backpack shifted.

Chemical bonding, I thought.

I knew why the doll had come to my chemistry class, and I knew why she'd brought the shattered pieces of her broken head.

I knew exactly what she wanted me to do.

⟨──⟩

All that day, she kept getting out of my backpack. In art class, I found her propped in my cubby. After lunch, she showed up on the floor of my locker. During Lab Rats, she even appeared along one wall, next to the Bunsen burners.

"Your doll prank wasn't even funny the first time you tried it," said Mia Lopez.

That afternoon, when I walked in the front door and dropped my backpack, I headed straight for the kitchen and grabbed a bottle of glue from the junk drawer.

Chemical bonding, I thought.

I took the doll to my bedroom and emptied the clear baggie onto my desk.

I started scientifically, of course. I laid the broken pieces out in rows. I separated the darker pieces, which I figured were her hair, and the lighter pieces, which had to be her skin. I found her two eyes and her nose and the three pieces that made up her mouth. I put those pieces in a row.

When I'd laid out everything, I counted.

There were forty-three pieces.

The biggest was the size of a dime. The smallest was just a sliver. I propped the doll on my desk, but before I went to work, I spoke to the doll for the first time ever.

"If I do this," I said, "you have to promise to leave me alone. You have to stop staring at me."

I waited.

I don't know what I expected to happen, but suddenly, the pieces with eyes on them seemed to flicker in the light. The familiar shudder washed over me—on my neck and my arms and everywhere—bigger than I'd ever felt it.

I guess that's an answer, I thought.

So I fingered the lighter-colored pieces.

I started looking for one that I could bond to her jagged neckline.

That first night, I worked for four hours. I found just two pieces that fit onto her neck.

Two. Out of forty-three.

The problem was that there were so many small pieces and so many jagged angles. I had to pick up a piece and place it on her neck, and then, when it didn't fit, I had to turn it and try it in a different spot.

I had to go through this process again and again until I was sure I'd found a perfect fit. Sometimes, I couldn't tell if a piece was exactly right or not, so I'd set it aside and keep looking.

I didn't want to glue anything until I was certain.

The next morning, when I woke up, she was on my pillow again, froofy and headless and not six inches away.

I opened my eyes, saw her there, and sprung out of my bed. I managed not to scream.

That day, she showed up on a shelf in the school library. She appeared in the backseat of Mom's Toyota. She was even there on the bathroom floor after my evening shower.

Imagine that—stepping out of the shower, wrapping a towel around yourself, and turning around to see a mostly headless doll propped against the closed bathroom door.

I remembered the second before I'd dropped her, when I'd thought that maybe I shouldn't do it, that maybe I should put her back on the mantel and walk away.

I wished I had.

Because over the next few weeks, she refused to leave me alone. She showed up on my back deck and in the kitchen pantry. I found her in my clothes hamper on laundry day and in my backpack before a big history test. Once, she appeared in the middle of a sidewalk I was walking down.

She seemed to be everywhere. Each time she appeared, I'd startle and steady my breathing.

She didn't seem to care that I was trying, that I was working to piece her back together.

I got jumpy, not knowing where she'd turn up next. The garage? The movie theater? The Lab Rats supply closet?

"What's your deal lately?" asked Mia Lopez at a Lab Rats meeting when I couldn't remember the difference between an acid and a base.

One night, I was working on her. I'd reconstructed her face almost up to her eyes, and I wanted a glass of juice. That was all. I left her for a second—only a second—and when I opened the fridge, there she was.

She was using a gallon of milk as a backrest.

I'm not kidding.

It'll be okay, I told myself as I grabbed her out of the fridge and stomped back to my room. I was making progress, and in one more week, I figured, I'd be finished. In one more week, I'd put her back on the mantel.

And I'd be free.

———

She wasn't going to look the same when I was done.

That was obvious.

I'd tried to make everything perfect, but cracks ran through her face and glue globbed up in a few places. It took me a long time to figure out that I could use a small paintbrush to smooth the glue before I attached a piece.

Despite all this, I hoped that when I was finished she'd keep her promise and leave me alone.

That's what I was thinking about one night as I sat at my desk and sifted through piece after piece of her ceramic hair.

Keep going, I told myself. *Just keep going.*

There was a knock on my door. It was Mom.

"She's looking creepier than ever," she said from the doorway. "Is it weird that I like her even more this way?"

I looked up.

"Mitchell," she said. "It's sweet that you're trying to fix the doll, but it's after midnight."

I blinked and I saw the cracked-headed doll in my locker, in my bathroom, in my chemistry class.

I wanted this to be over.

I wanted her to leave me alone.

"Just one more piece," I said, picking up a tiny porcelain shard from my desk.

Mom nodded. "One more piece," she said. "Then you sleep."

After I'd placed that piece, though, I kept working.

I found another piece. And another one.

I felt like a kind of machine. I'd place a piece, hold it till the glue dried, reach absently for another piece, and then do it all again.

Hours passed.

My eyes ached and my head drooped.

But I kept going.

And little by little, the doll's head came together.

Soon, around four in the morning, all that was left was the tiniest hole in the doll's face. It was a gap over her right eye, no bigger than a pencil eraser.

I was going to do it. I was going to finish.

One more piece, I thought.

I reached absently for the final piece, but I didn't feel anything where I'd lined up the shards on my desk. Just a smooth wooden surface.

Where was the last piece?

My desk was bare except for the doll and my glue and the plastic baggie I'd emptied out weeks ago. I picked it up and shook it.

It was empty.

A hole opened up inside me, like the hole in the doll's face.

I got down on the floor. Where could the last piece be? I squinted. It had to be somewhere. We'd swept up all the pieces. Mom and Dad and I. I'd even checked the living room floor myself.

I stopped.

No, I remembered. *I hadn't.*

Mom and Dad had looked for scattered pieces. But not me. Not really.

I ran down the dark hallway to the living room. I switched on the light and I knelt and peered under the couches and along the baseboards.

I didn't find anything.

How many times had we vacuumed since I'd dropped the doll?

Then she appeared—just like that—on the floor by my left hand. Her too-realistic eyes seemed to narrow, and I felt the cold, familiar shudder—on my neck and arms and everywhere.

My eyes darted up and down the hard oak planks.

"I'll find it," I told her. "Give me a minute and I'll find it."

Where could the last piece be?

The vacuum bag? The garbage can? The county dump?

The cold shudder was coming in waves now.

"Please." I looked at the doll. "You have to understand."

Her eyes dug into me. The hole in her face turned pitch-black, like a tiny sliver of night.

I started breathing fast. I didn't know what to do next.

I needed to find that piece.

If I didn't, she'd never leave me alone. If I didn't, she'd keep on following me forever. If I didn't, we'd be connected . . . fused . . . permanently . . .

Chemically bonded.

THE
Heartbeat
A BEDTIME STORY

IT'S your own, you think—the heartbeat you hear when your head's on the pillow.

Thu-thump, thu-thump, thu-thump.

It must be, you tell yourself as your breathing slows and your thoughts grow foggy and dim. It's just your own pulse, beating in your inner ear. You've heard it a thousand times.

Thu-thump, thu-thump.

That sound. It is your own blood coursing through your own veins. That's what you believe—what you need to be true. It's the one thing that lets you keep breathing slowly, lets you keep drifting deeper.

Thu-thump.

What else could it be, this pounding?

From where else could it come?

So you drift, your unsuspecting head settling deeper into the warm, full pillow.

Thu-thump.

You don't worry.

Why would you?

You know nothing of the truth. Nothing of your pillow's true intentions. Nothing of its dark and pulsing heart, throbbing in your ears.

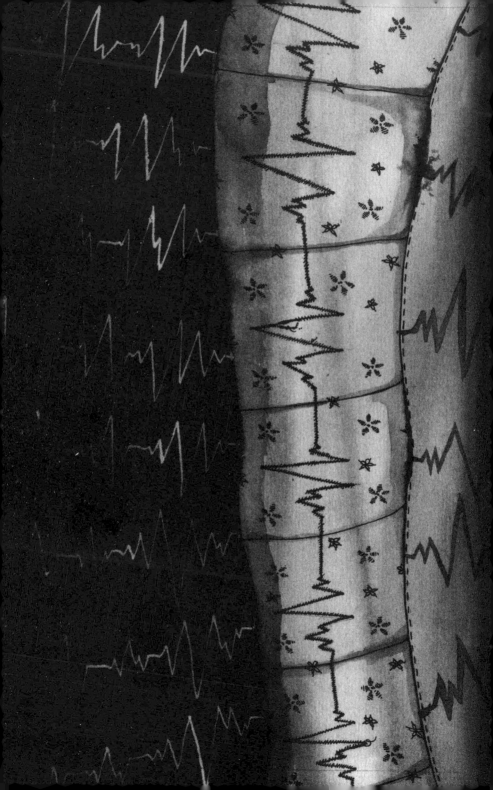

Thu-thump.

You know nothing of its aching hunger, which has seethed and swelled for years, and which, tonight, can wait no more. It's been so patient.

Thu-thump, thu-thump.

So you know nothing of this moment, of how your pillow's billowing folds now rise on either side of your head, now balloon higher and higher as you settle deeper, and now wait . . . poised to do their menacing work, to surround and smother and suffocate while you thrash and kick and flail, if only you will drift a little deeper, if only you will sleep once more.

Which, with a long exhale, you do.

Thu-thump, thu-thump, thu-thump.

ACKNOWLEDGMENTS

I owe many thanks to the good people at Holiday House Books for believing in these stories. Most especially, I'm indebted to Sally Morgridge, my remarkably talented editor, whose guidance has made me a better writer. Thank you, Sally. I'm also indebted to Terry Borzumato-Greenberg, Emily Mannon, and Elizabeth Law. Thank you, each of you, for your stellar work and your remarkable kindness.

I'm immensely lucky to have such a good friend and gifted agent in Rick Margolis. Never have I worked with a kinder, gentler soul.

I would not be a writer today if it weren't for the support of my colleagues at BYU-Idaho. Thank you, Jason Williams, Mark Bennion, Jack Harrell, Suzette Kunz, Kristen Glenn, and Paula Soper. I'm honored to know each of you. Thank you, also, Steve Stewart, not only for your unfailing support, but also for assigning your professional writing class to read an early draft of this book and give me such thoughtful advice. And thank you to each of those students for your dedicated work.

Thank you also to the many teachers and librarians who've welcomed me into their schools over the years. I'm especially thankful to Patti Zimmerman, Beth Clovis, and Jennifer Robinson.

I am deeply indebted to fourth-grade teacher Tricia Galer and her students from Madison Middle School in Rexburg, Idaho. These students listened to early drafts of these stories, and their support means more than they'll ever know. They are Greyson Abel, Adam Erikson, Ella Erickson, Samuel Furness, Malcolm Hopkins, Sophia Hyde, Bradley Isle, Scarlett Kerr, Joshua Mckay, Corban McKinney, Cadence Mecham, Maxwell Mounts, Kelsey Munns, Dylan Payne, Brooklyn Redd, Isaac Ricks, Henry Stewart, Capri Tighe, Ryker Trickey, Ellie Ray Wiggins, and Jacob Williams.

I'm blessed to know Greg and Tiffany Nielson at Idaho Book Fairs. Thank you for the lovely work you do, and thank you for helping me share my stories with so many kids.

I'm beyond thrilled that Sarah J. Coleman and I have now collaborated on two books together. There's no illustrator I'd want to work with more. Thank you, Sarah, for your beautifully spooky artwork. Let's meet in person someday, shall we?

Finally, I owe my family—my kids, my parents, and most especially, my wife, Suzy—more thanks than I can ever offer. This book exists—I exist—because of you.

I love you all.